ROYAL Blood

Written by Claire C. Riley

Cover design by Constant of Wilde Designs

Please note.

This story was originally written in 2019 as part of the Blazing Gun's anthology which was on sale for three months. The story has since been re-written and fully expanded upon.

ROYAL BLOOD
The Brotherhood

PLAYLIST

You? – Two Feet

Break My Baby – Kaleo

Be Your Love – Bishop Briggs

You & Me – Yelawolf

Cover Me in Sunshine – Pink, Willow Sage Hart

Perfect Day – Tundra Beats

Runaway – Aurora

'Till I Collapse – Eminem feat Nate Dogg

Salt – B.Miles

Let You Go – Illenium feat. Ember Island

Sunset Lover – Petit Biscuit

Creep – Ember Island

Fire – Two Feet

Available on Apple music

https://music.apple.com/gb/playlist/royal-blood-the-
brotherhood-playlist/pl.u-MREJTYboDq

ROYAL BLOOD: THE BROTHERHOOD

A Reverse Harem Mafia Romance

Natalia has always known that she was promised to a man 25 years her senior. However, after the Novello brothers, come to the aid of her father Frank, everything changes. Frank is king of the underworld. The Don of NYC. He has money, drugs, guns, thriving businesses and half the police force under his belt. So when he offers the brothers payment for helping him, he's surprised when the only thing they demand is Natalia.

Unable to refuse their offer, Frank reluctantly hands over his only daughter to the Novello brothers and a war breaks out between the three families.

When duty and jealousy collide, the flames of temptation are fanned and the only thing standing in the way of bloodshed and war is the promise of seduction from the virgin daughter of Frank Costello.

Can there ever be life after the Brotherhood take their payment from her? Or does the ultimate betrayal lie in her own blood?

Blood ROYAL

THE BROTHERHOOD
A Reverse Harem Mafia Romance

BY
USA TODAY BESTSELLING AUTHOR
CLAIRE C RILEY

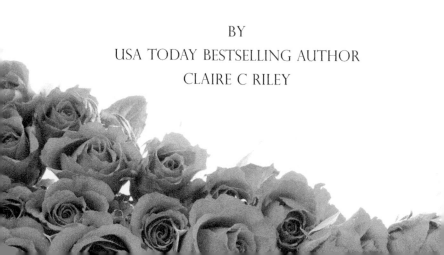

Prologue

Dominic

I'd rather be the hunter than the prey.

Who wants to be a mouse when you can be a wolf? With sharp teeth and a taste for blood, there's nothing in this world that would make me ever bow to another person.

I'm a Novello and I've been raised to be anything but a pussy. Blood, violence, and vengeance have surrounded me since I was a boy and were intravenously fed to me while still in my mother's belly.

I'm a menace to society.

I'm a monster.

The thing you run from on a dark night.

I'm everything your parents warned you about.

Cracking my neck from side to side, I stare down into

Romy Edmunds's bloody face. His eyes are so swollen they don't open, blood drooling from between puffy lips, hair slick with blood and sweat and God knows what else. I grip his graying hair in my hand and raise his face up to me, giving a shake of my head.

He's done.

I release his hair and his head drops, his chin hitting his chest as a wretched sob leaves him. He's done and he knows he's done. Fucker should be glad that I'm too furious to take my time and string his death out for months.

Angelo, the head of my security, hands me a small towel to wipe my bloody hands with and I take it gratefully. I didn't have to get my hands bloody tonight. That is, after all, why I have him around now—to do the grunt work while I give off the illusion of a respectful business owner. But this shit needed to be handled by me and me alone.

Joey and Sisco are gonna be pissed at me for taking this on myself, but for once I don't give a shit about their opinion. This needed to be done. Tonight. By me.

Romy Edmunds murdered my father, the don of the Novellos and one of the three kings of New York City. He murdered him and then left his body on our doorstep for my mother to find. A warning. I still don't know who gave the order to send him down, but I will.

I won't rest until I find out, and neither will my brothers.

Now it's just us—three vengeful brothers, one little

sister, and a heartbroken mother with no memory of us most of the time.

But we're the Novellos, and this is a new time now. With my father gone, we've taken over the kingdom, his empire, his life's work. Things will be changing, heads will be rolling, and money will be flowing.

I pull out my gun and aim it at Romy's head.

This death is too good for him, but hatred is pumping through my veins and I want him dead and gone before morning breaks. Before Sisco or Joey find out and try to extract their own anger on this piece of shit.

I'm the middle son, with Sisco being the eldest, however he's always been unstable, and Joey is too fucking smart for this life. He shouldn't have to get his hands bloody.

No, this is my responsibility as the dutiful and loyal son of Michael Novella. I'm going to honor his memory and find the bastard that killed him. And when I do, they'll wish they'd killed my entire fucking family with the amount of wrath I'm going to rain down on them.

"One last chance, Romy. Tell me who ordered the hit," I say, my voice cold as steel.

He chokes on his own blood, half sobbing as he tries to get his words out. "I'm a dead man if I te—"

"Does this look like a fucking water pistol to you?" I roar, my fury getting the better of me. I bend one knee and put my face up to his, pressing the gun to his temple.

"You're a dead man either way, Romy, but I'll let you choose the quickest route out, because believe me when I say you do not want Sisco to find you still breathing. This pain that you're in right now, it is nothing compared to what he will put you through. He'll keep you alive for years, torturing you. Cutting parts of you off and feeding them back to you. I'm being kind. I'll make it quick."

I'm breathing hard, my chest heaving. I want to beat him until he's nothing but blood and bones, the life torn from him limb by limb. Rage and sorrow burn through my body, the screams of my little sister forever scorched into my brain.

"Tell me," I say through gritted teeth.

Romy's breathing sounds painful and labored, rasps of air leaving his lungs.

"Okay," he says.

I lower the gun from his temple and put my face next to his, listening to the name that spills from his bloody lips.

I pat him on the shoulder when he is done.

"You did good," I say, standing back up. "And I am a man of my word."

I aim the gun again and pull the trigger. The bullet hits Romy in the center of his forehead and he falls sideways, dead and gone. Lucky son of a bitch. He didn't deserve that death. He deserved death from Sisco, but I am a man of my word, and a promise is a promise.

I hand the gun off to Angelo, who wipes it down and puts it away. He'll dispose of it for me once he gets rid of Romy's body.

"I need to get back. My brothers will be wondering where I am," I say, and head back to my blacked-out limo.

I don't need to tell Angelo what needs to be done next; he already knows. He's worked with me long enough and I trust him with my life.

Once in the limo my driver pulls away, taking me back to the home I share with my family. I have an apartment in the city, but we've all been staying at the mansion since my father was brutally murdered. My mother and sister need us with them.

Our family needs to be stronger than ever now.

Our bond tight, our loyalty unquestionable.

I'll hunt down the man who participated in the murder of my father.

One by one I'll take them all out.

One by one, they'll all pay.

But tonight we mourn the loss of him.

My driver heads through the darkened streets of NYC, threading through the light traffic toward our family home. I'm ready for Joey and Sisco to give me shit about doing this without them. I'm ready to take on the tears of my little sister and the broken memories of my mother.

I'm ready for it all.

Chapter 1

Natalia

I stare at my reflection in the floor-length mirror. My shimmery gold dress clings to every curve of my body, accentuating the hourglass figure my mother's DNA blessed me with.

Tonight is the night my father is going to give his blessing to the marriage between me and Alfonso Rosso, a man of incredible power and authority. A man that has been at the sidelines of my life since birth. We've barely ever shared more than a handful of words up until these last few months, but I've always known what was coming—what must happen. And he's waited so patiently for me.

"You should be more grateful," my mother says from behind me. Her wedding to my father happened when she was 17 and he was 37. She'd had no choice either. It was her duty, as this is mine.

I try to drown out her words, because I don't want to hear this story again. It's the one she's told me since my sixteenth birthday: She didn't love my father but she did what needed to be done for the sake of her family. She learned to love my father eventually and everything worked out for the best for everyone.

I get it.

I do.

I just don't like it.

I want to marry for love, not duty.

I don't want to be bound by honoring my family and marrying a man twice my age.

I want the flutters of love and desire. First dates, stolen kisses, promises of forever.

I've never even kissed a man before because my body and soul has been promised to Alfonso.

But there's no point in arguing about it again. My fate has been sealed and I have accepted it.

Mother comes up behind me, the scent of white wine and her sickly perfume mixing into one and making me feel even more nauseous than I already do.

She's drunk again. She's always drunk, but today she started earlier than usual. I think she's scared for me. Certainly nervous for me. She doesn't really like this any more than I do, but she has no choice in the matter either.

I hate her for not saying something.

For not fighting for me.

"You're so beautiful, Natalia," she coos, her hand stroking my long dark hair. Her eyes are glazed and her fingers tremble. She looks at me in the mirror and smiles.

"Thank you, Mother." I force a smile back, giving her what she wants. "I get all my looks from you, of course."

She lifts her chin higher, her own gaze going from me to herself as she admires her own reflection. "We come from good stock."

Good stock. I want to laugh. She talks like we're merely cattle, being bought and sold off at a farmer's market. If we were cattle, her statement would be true because we do come from good stock.

Smooth, tanned skin, long dark hair, blue eyes, slender bodies. I'm as beautiful as my mother was before the alcohol and drugs ravaged said beauty. I think that's why she hates me too. I am what she once was, what she longs to still be. And she knows I will end up just like her.

My mother is a tiny Italian woman with a mischievous smile. Right now she uses that smile on me.

"He's a good strong man, Natalia," she says, her eyes back on me in the mirror. I don't know who she's trying to convince, her or me. I know all about Alfonso Rosso, and he is anything but good.

"I know," I agree. And I do. Not so much about the good part, because I don't think any man that my father knows is a typically good man, but he is a strong man. He'll provide for me, protect me, and all I have to do is be a dutiful wife and provide him with an heir.

She steps back and examines me in my dress, making sure that I'm looking every bit the perfect wife-to-be. She sighs and seems dissatisfied with my appearance, but we both know I look good. My dress is long and tight, clinging to my ample curves. I wanted to wear black, but she was insistent that I wear gold. It's cut low down the front, pushing my breasts up high and accentuating them. A long split around the thigh area shows off my legs. I feel like a cow on show, baring my assets to the richest farmer!

Her eyes narrow. "You don't know how lucky you are. You could do so much worse than Alfonso Rosso, Natalia. At least your father chose someone attractive! I never had such luck." She laughs bitterly. "You're one of the fortunate ones."

I make a noise in the back of my throat and she spins me round to look at her, her hand raising to slap my cheek. "I'm sorry," I say immediately. "I just . . . it doesn't matter."

"No, go on, say it!" she bites out angrily, her palm itching to strike me.

I decide it's now or never. One last chance to save myself from this fate, even though I know it's pointless.

"It's just that he's so much older than me, Mother." I chew the inside of my cheek, already wishing I wouldn't have bothered saying anything. No one cares what I think or what I want. It's never been a decision I could make. And truthfully, I don't care about his age anyway. I just don't want him.

"Alfonso will give you everything you need in life."

"But not love," I interrupt.

"This is business!" she snaps, suddenly furious with me. "Love?" she scoffs. "Silly girl, who needs love when you have money, power, respect! Be satisfied that your father picked as strong a man as Alfonso Rosso and not some lowlife for you."

"But Mother . . ."

"No!" she screeches. "You will marry him. Your father promised you to him when you were six months old. It's a contract. A deal. And you will be respectful and follow through with his wishes."

Tears fill my eyes and my chin quivers. How can she do this? How can she agree to this? My father is a scary man, but he loves her, and me. If she just spoke to him, he might listen to her.

"But I want to marry for something greater than power and money. I want love," I plead.

My mother laughs. "Love? What do you know of love? If we all married for love we'd be whores on the street, child.

Your father and I know best. You will marry Alfonso and you will be satisfied!"

I'm about to argue more with her when there's a knock on the door and Mary, my nursemaid, comes in. I close my mouth and swallow my protests. It's futile anyway.

"Gah, Natalia, look at you!" Mary gasps, her hands clasping before her as she takes in me and the tension between my mother and me.

I blush. "It's just the dress," I say shyly.

Mary says something in French that I don't understand and comes forward, busying herself at my dressing table. She's an older woman, plump around the middle with a hard face that never betrays her true feelings.

"You are beautiful and Mr. Rosso is a very lucky man." She says his name with obvious distaste. She doesn't want this marriage, this bonding, any more than I do. But like me, she's bound by obligation and would never dare utter a word against my father's decision.

"Isn't he just," my mother coos. She heads to the door. "I'll see you down there. Don't keep your father waiting." She pulls her masquerade mask back on as she slips out of the room, her long, sequined dress trailing behind her.

Mary clicks the door closed behind her and comes to me, pulling me into a strong hug. Mary doesn't do delicate or gentle. She's not sensitive or quiet. Her hugs are strong, her words fierce, and her meaning always blatant.

I return the hug and she pats my back before pulling out of the hug and looking me dead in the eye. "How are we doing? And don't give me any nonsense about being fine." She air quotes fine and I smile.

"Nervous, I guess." I shrug. "It is what it is though."

She mutters something in French again. "It's wrong is what it is. A beauty like you shouldn't be married off to a man his age. It's wrong. Dégoûtant!"

I smile and shrug again. "I'll be fine. He's a fine man. Strong, honorable. I'll want for nothing, and it will make my father happy. It will keep the business going." I turn back to my reflection and pick up the diamond hair slide before handing it to Mary. "Will you?"

She nods and takes it from me before sliding it into my hair. "Je trouve toujours ça dégoûtant!"

She pulls my hair over one shoulder, giving me a firm eye up and down before nodding in satisfaction. I pull on my mask and take one last look at myself, satisfied with what stares back at me.

"It's time," I say with dread.

Royal Blood

The party is in full swing. My father, Frank Costello, has turned 65 and half of New York City has turned up to help him celebrate. A mountain of gifts carefully wrapped in expensive paper sits in the corner of the room, next to an enormous cake in the shape of the Empire State Building. A weird homage to the place my father signed his first dirty cop onto his payroll.

Everyone is either dancing or eating, talking or drinking. Everyone is celebrating. Everyone barring me. Despite what I know must happen, I've been avoiding my mother, father, and Alfonso Rosso for most of the night, choosing to spend my time in the library, away from the party and my duty. I guess you could say I'm just trying to enjoy my last night of freedom by myself.

I'm reading a book when I hear the door open and confident footsteps come in. The library is off-limits to party guests, hence why I came in here. I slip my mask back on and put the book down before standing up.

"Hello?" I say out loud when I don't immediately see anyone. "Who's there?" My voice is soft but I hold my nerve, despite the uncomfortable feeling crawling up my spine.

"Not the sociable type either?" A voice comes from behind one of the shelving units, and I step around, coming face to face with the speaker. He's tall and dark, his deep brown eyes demanding my attention and threatening violence. Something is frightening about him, like a lit

13

firework seconds away from exploding, and yet I find him both attractive and intriguing. "I find these things so pretentious, don't you? What's good about growing old? One year closer to death, I say." He laughs and raises his glass in the air.

I frown. "It's supposed to be a celebration of life."

He barks out a laugh. "Life, death, it's all the same. They're intrinsically connected. Celebrating your life while getting closer to your death." He scoffs and takes a sip of his drink.

His brown hair is swept back from his face, a slight curve near his ears like his hair is naturally unruly and he's made a feeble attempt at taming it tonight. He looks down at the book I'd put down, raising an eyebrow.

"Little Women? Also pretentious."

I look down at it and then back to him, perplexed by his boldness. I'm the princess of Frank Costello and no man normally dares talk to me, never mind mock my choice of books. I'd say as much, but he seems a little scary, even for one of my father's friends.

"You should read Dr. Jekyll and Mr. Hyde. It's still pretentious but it's worth the read for its darkness alone," he says. "'You must suffer me to go my own dark way,'" he continues with a sneer before finishing off his drink. "Woman like you, no doubt you've already read it, am I right?"

I don't have time to reply as the door swings open wider

and another man comes in, his broad shoulders filling the doorway.

"Sisco, where the fuck have you been?" He stops in his tracks when he sees me standing there. His features are stern, like a father about to give a lecture to his son, but he's clearly younger than the other man named Sisco. "I need to steal my brother away for a moment, love. You should get back to the party."

I frown. "I should, should I?" I smart, annoyed by the arrogance of these two men.

"Yes," he replies with a hard edge, as if annoyed by my audacity to answer back. "There's a glass of champagne with your name on it out there, I'm sure."

He's being condescending, just like all men. 'The silly little girl doesn't know how to think for herself. Give her champagne and a pretty dress and she'll be happy.' Anger flares in my chest, and it must show on my face too because he smirks, holding my gaze and daring me to voice my bitter thoughts.

"I was finished anyway," the man named Sisco replies. He winks at me, the corner of his mouth pulling up in a slanted grin as he walks away.

I have the urge to order them both out of my home, but I know my father wouldn't stand for it. This is his night. These are his guests. And I am merely a pawn to him. I don't have any say, tonight or any other night.

"Until next time," Sisco says as I glare at them both.

When they've both left, I look down at the book I was reading before picking it up and putting it back on the shelf. I move along the bookcase until I find Dr. Jekyll and Mr. Hyde and pull it down. A first edition that my father bought for me when I was barely twelve years old. It had cost him thousands, no doubt. He's right, I have read it before, yet the words I read never sounded as dark and as menacing as the ones he just quoted, despite me knowing what happens in the book.

"Natalia?" Mary's voice screeches from the hallway, and I sigh and put the book back. I guess it was time I spent some time with my future husband.

Chapter 2

Dominic

"What the fuck were you doing in there?" I snap as Sisco and I head back to the bullshit party we're at.

None of us want to be here, but duty means we have to. Frank Costello is turning 65, and for a mob boss that's pretty fucking good. Anyone who is anyone is here, and with my brothers and me stepping into my father's shoes, it means I've shaken hands with more powerful men of the mafia underworld than ever before. It's the sort of place my father would have normally come to, but now that duty has befallen his sons.

Sisco shrugs, giving me a sly grin. "You know me, I'm like a missile for a pretty girl."

"I just need you to not be an asshole tonight. We've got bigger things to be thinking about than women." We enter the large room where the party is being held, and I scan it, looking for Joey. "For God's sake, I told him to stay here." I drag a hand through my hair, feeling the beginnings of a headache coming on.

"All work and no play makes Sisco . . ."

"Do not finish that sentence, brother," I warn. "I am not in the mood. Did you take your meds before we came out?"

Sisco rolls his eyes and nods. He's the eldest brother, but it's me that's taken over the bulk of our father's work, since Sisco is all hands and no head when it comes to this business. He serves our family well when it comes to things getting bloody, but not all mafia business is blood. A lot of it takes more finesse than that, something that he just doesn't have.

I'm feeling the pressure from every angle right now. The stress of keeping my family safe, together, and wealthy. Business is good, and since my father's murder we've had crime lords from every district coming out to pay their respects and offering their services to us. Whether that be to make new deals or hide their crime from me, I'm not sure. But everyone is a suspect right now and I'm taking no chances.

I move away from the party with Sisco at my heels, and head towards the kitchen. Joey is like Sisco and he can't seem to keep his head in the game right now. Chasing women is what he's always done, and if he can find a gem in the rough then that's where he'll be.

Pushing open the large wooden door that leads to the kitchen, I search for Joey, thinking that he's no doubt been chasing down one of the maids or the waitresses. The scent of rich foods invades my senses and my stomach rumbles in response. I haven't eaten properly in weeks and it's catching up to me. Instead of eating I've been working out, trying to get rid of the extra tension in my muscles. My body is chiseled and firm, muscles upon muscles. So much so that I've had to order new suits. Which doesn't come cheap, since I have expensive taste.

I should cut back or go easy. Sisco is right—all work and no play isn't good for anyone. But I can't sleep, I can't eat, I can't even fuck without thinking of vengeance. Without hearing my little sister crying for my father. Without seeing the sneering faces of the men who had the fucking audacity to think they could get away with killing my father. Without seeing my father's blood dried upon the steps of his home.

So, I train and I work.

I sweat and I shower.

I run and down a smoothie.

I do a hundred push-ups, forcing my muscles to breaking point, and then I take an ice bath.

I'm rebuilding myself from the inside out.

They say change is good for the soul, but my soul was almost nonexistent in the first place, so who knows who I'll be at the end of this.

I don't see Joey at first, and I'm about to walk out when I hear something. "Joey?"

"I'm here," he grunts.

Sisco and I move around the kitchen, finding him on the ground, his hands in the center of another man's chest. I recognize the man immediately. It's Frank Costello and he's unconscious. He looks pale as hell and I worry that he might already be dead.

"Jesus Christ," I mutter. "What did you do?"

"Can you get down here and help me?" he grunts, pressing his hands into Frank's chest once more.

"This your doing?" Sisco laughs, not giving a shit about the drama unfolding in front of us, or the repercussions of Franks demise.

"Help me," Joey says more urgently, his hands locked together as he presses on Frank's chest. "I don't know how long he's been out. I came in to—"

"Find some feathers?" Sisco laughs, and I cringe at the ridiculous slang name they both use for maids. Despite the situation, Joey smirks.

"Yes, but then I found him here instead. Not the good time I was hoping for."

I turn to Sisco. "Call an ambulance, now!" I shove

him toward the door and head over to help Joey. "What happened, little brother?"

Joey is doing CPR on Frank, his features tight as he concentrates. He shakes his head. "I don't know. I told you, I found him on the ground like this."

His sleeves are rolled up, his suit jacket under Frank's head. He leans over, pinches Frank's nose, and blows into his mouth before continuing with the compressions. The kitchen door swings back open and I hear the footsteps of several panicked people coming in.

"Frank!" a woman cries, dropping to her knees beside us. She's clearly drunk and she crowds the man, pulling on his shirt and sobbing uncontrollably like her own life depends on it.

Jesus Christ, someone needs to get her under control.

"Father?" a girl's voice calls, but I don't look up. All my attention is on Frank and Joey and the hysterical woman. I take over the compressions as Joey pinches Frank's nose again and blows into his mouth.

There are too many people in the kitchen and they're all getting closer and closer, all wanting to take a look at the great Frank Costello unconscious on the floor. The great king of New York knocking on deaths door. Normally I wouldn't give a shit, but I get an image of my own father on the ground, men gathered around him as he was beaten to death. Their leers staring down at him, unsympathetic, uncaring. Ambivalent towards his pain.

These violent delights have violent ends.

"Get back and give us some goddamn space!" I roar, needing the space for me more than just Frank. "Is the ambulance on its way?"

"Any minute now," a man says, and when I look up I see one of Frank's security guys. He looks worried, and he should be. Frank holds the keys to the kingdom, and with no son to pass his empire down to, the vultures will be coming to tear the Costello's apart if Frank dies.

Minutes that feel like hours pass until finally paramedics arrive, but another man is holding them back and not allowing them to come in. Sisco is arguing with whoever it is; I can hear his angry voice from my place on the ground and I know it's only minutes before he really loses his shit.

"What the fuck is going on?" I yell at him.

Sisco barges in, violence written all over his face like vibrant graffiti. He doesn't give a shit about Frank, but he loves a good fight and he's hoping this will end that way.

"Some asshole is keeping the medics back. He thinks it's a hit," Sisco sneers. "I told him it will be a fucking hit on him if he doesn't let them in."

How has this descended into such chaos?

"You, take over," I order Frank's security man.

The big guy drops to his knees and takes over from me.

I storm to the doorway to sort this shit out, more than a

little pissed off now. A man I know to be Alfonso Rosso, or Alfonso, is holding the paramedics back. I tap him on the shoulder, and when he turns around, I glare. "Let them in, now," I order, giving no room for him to argue with me, and yet he does.

He sneers at me, clearly not used to being told what to do. He's older than me, but he looks after himself. His large shoulders fill out the expensive suit he wears. "And you are?"

"Your worst fucking nightmare if you don't get out of their way. He's had a heart attack and needs to get to a hospital, so unless you want to be the man that kills off Frank Costello, I suggest you get the fuck out of their way."

He takes a step forward, his gaze looking me up and down like he owns me, like he's better than me. I should pull out my gun and kill him for the disrespect, but the whole point of coming here tonight was to make new business contacts, not kill them off.

Satisfied he's won the cock show, he takes a step back and allows the paramedics in, his gaze never leaving mine. I can feel Sisco at my side, tension pouring from him like wine from a broken bottle. He's like a vicious rottweiler ready to be unleashed, eager and hungry for blood. But unlike my father, God rest his soul, I refuse to use Sisco's anger as a weapon.

I hold out my hand to Alfonso. "Dominic Novello."

Alfonso looks at my hand, a smile creeping up his face.

The man is older than me by a good ten years, his silver-flecked hair the only sign since he's had so much Botox.

"Stay out of my way," Alfonso orders, and pushes past me and into the kitchen.

"I'm going to kill him for that," Sisco growls, his hand reaching for the gun at his waist as Joey comes out of the kitchen.

His features darken when he sees Sisco's expression, and I know he's already on board for murder if I agree.

I place a hand on Sisco's arm. "Not tonight, brother."

Sisco seems even more infuriated by my response. Or lack of one. "You're going to let him disrespect you like that?"

I start to walk and my brothers follow. When we're out of earshot, I turn to them. "There's more than one way to kill a snake, and I'm in it for the long game."

Joey nods. He's the sensible one. He can take orders. But Sisco, he's wild, uncontrollable. Like a 50-year storm he destroys everything in his path. He's going to take a little more convincing.

"Brother, if we went around killing everyone we disliked, we'd have no one to do business with. We need to be smart about this. Our name looks weak right now. Our own father was murdered and dropped on our doorstep, for Christ's sakes. We need to show everyone that we're more than just brawn, that we can use our fucking heads and take over what he left behind."

I watch as Frank is wheeled out of the kitchen, a mask secured over his mouth. He's still out cold, but I can see the faint rise and fall of his chest. Frank's security team works on getting rid of the guests despite his drunk wife's insistence that he'd want the party to continue. Nothing like love and loyalty to turn my stomach sour.

"Let's get out of here," I say, and we head out to our waiting limo.

As we climb inside, I see the woman that Sisco had been talking to. Her arms are wrapped around her body to keep herself warm as she watches them load Frank into a waiting ambulance. She's been crying and smudges of mascara dirty her damp cheeks. She's sexy as hell, even with tear-stained cheeks. Maybe even because of them. She's not the sort of woman I'd normally go for though. She seems shy and reserved. The epitome of a good Catholic daughter. I like my women to have more fight in them than that. I like them dirty and bent over my knee with my cock in their mouth. This woman would crumble at the first sign of seduction.

Alfonso comes out of the building, his cell phone to his ear. He scans the crowd, his features pulled tight with irritation. Finally, he spots what he's looking for and he makes a beeline for the woman. She visibly flinches as he comes closer to her, lowering her gaze to her feet. It all becomes clear to me who she is. She's Frank's daughter. The one he promised to Alfonso when she was firstborn.

It's not an uncommon practice—arranged marriage—and most women are happy enough to go through with it. And why wouldn't they be? Their fathers choose a man from a powerful family, one of wealth and importance. The woman never wants for anything. But this woman, Frank's daughter, visibly shudders as Alfonso drapes a heavy arm across her shoulders.

In this life, nothing is given for free.

Not respect, or money, or power.

Yet Frank has clearly tried to seal that in her future.

It's a damn shame really. She's striking. A classic beauty with a figure that makes my dick harder than steel. I haven't thought about women or sex since the morning my little sister phoned me, hysterical, because our father was mutilated on the doorstep, but something had clicked back on when I walked into the library and saw her with Sisco. It's true; she's not my type but breaking her would be enjoyable to say the least.

"Well, that party sucked," Joey laughs. "Are we heading out for drinks?"

He's only twenty-four and unfazed by everything in life. He barely shed a tear after our own father's death. He's cold and calculated with not a drop of empathy for anyone. He deals with everything in life as a transaction. He's like our father in many ways. One man's death is another man's gain.

"No," I reply sharply. "We promised Eva we'd go straight home."

He nods despite being unhappy about the decision. Sisco pulls out a small flask from his inside pocket and takes a long drink, determined to have a party for one if need be.

My driver automatically takes a left upon hearing this, and I press a button and the partition goes up. My brothers turn to look at me, their expressions serious.

My brothers.

My crazy, fucked-up, bloodthirsty brothers.

"What is it?" Joey asks, pouring himself a drink from the minibar.

"Something felt off tonight, don't you think?" I say.

"Yeah, you interrupted me with that fine piece of ass in the library," Sisco laughs, always the asshole.

I shake my head. "That was Frank's daughter."

"So?"

"Get your head back in the game, brother. We've bigger things to think about than getting your dick wet," I bark, irritated by him. "Besides, she's taken."

His cocky smile falls at my reprimand and I continue.

"Half of the underworld was there tonight. It was a show for them. Frank Costello may be sixty-five, but he's still got a lot of life left in him."

"Only he doesn't," Joey adds, and Sisco grunts in agreement.

Sisco is a great people reader. It's like a sixth sense to him. We all have our strengths and weaknesses, and this is one of his.

"He was arguing with someone just before I walked in," Joey continues. "Could be the argument triggered a heart attack." He shrugs and sits back, sipping his drink as he thinks.

"Maybe," I agree, but something still feels off. Not that any of this should matter to me. I have enough of my own shit to be dealing with as it is. And why should I care about Frank Costello? He was nothing to me...only, that's not entirely true. He was there at our father's funeral and he promised that he would reach out to all of his connections and find out if they knew anything.

I didn't trust anyone in this world, barring my family, but there had been a sense of sincerity in Frank's proposal.

I look over at Sisco and see him staring out the window, deep in thought.

"What is it, brother?"

"I hate all those pricks," he says, his mood darkening. "One of them killed him."

Joey pours Sisco a drink and he takes it, downing it in one go.

"I want them to pay."

"And they will," I promise.

Sisco looks over at me, his features drawn in anger,

but he nods in agreement, believing my every word. As he should. I will get vengeance for his murder. No matter the cost.

"Like I said, we're in this for the long game. I want to weed out the weak links, and then I'll take the bastards head."

He watched me thoughtfully, and for a moment I thought he was going to question me further. Perhaps disbelieving of me, but then he leaned forwards, elbows resting on his knees.

"Can I take their head, brother?" he asked.

Joey barked out a laugh and I felt my mouth quirk in amusement.

He wasn't bullshitting either.

He meant in the very literal sense.

"Absolutely," I readily agreed.

Chapter 3

Natalia

"**D**olcezza," Alfonso coos, waking me, his Italian accent accentuating each letter like he's trying to seduce me with the endearment.

I stir, my eyes fluttering open. I'm still at my father's bedside, and don't intend on leaving until I know that he's okay. I might hate the things he does, but he's still my father and I love him. I know he only wants the best for me. A better life than he had. The doctors said it was a heart attack, brought on by stress and alcohol. That sounds about right for my father.

Alfonso strokes a hand down my back, and it takes everything in me not to shrug off his touch. He stayed with me all night, refusing to give me even a moment's peace.

The thought of a lifetime of his torment makes me feel physically sick, though I don't know why. He's been nothing but nice to me.

"Can I get you anything?" he asks, his hand still stroking my back.

I sit up, feeling grateful when his hand reluctantly slides away. I look up and offer him a polite smile. "Coffee, please, Mr. Rosso."

His smile grows. "I think we can drop the formalities now, Natalia. Frank may not have been able to formally declare our impending marriage, but it is our future." He leans down and takes my hand before pulling it up to his mouth and kissing the back of it. "And what a wonderful marriage we shall have, cara mia."

His gaze drops to my cleavage, and I once again curse my mother for making me wear this thing.

"Very well, Alfonso. Coffee would be wonderful, please." I force the words out. I hate the sound of his name on my tongue. The feel of it in my mouth. How am I going to marry him when I can barely say his name without wanting to be sick? How can I endure a lifetime with this man when his very presence makes me shudder?

Is this why my own mother turned to drink? Did she never love my father? Did she drink to get through the long days and even longer nights? To endure my father between her thighs. Is this why they only had one child?

"I'll be right back. Donny is outside, so you will be safe," Alfonso says as he releases my hand and leaves the room, and I sigh with relief, my shoulders sagging. Tears prickle my eyes, but I wipe them away before they have a chance to fall.

I stand and walk to the window, looking out upon New York City and wondering if there is a way for a woman like me to escape. To hide from my obligations and future. The tears come again, and I sniffle and brush them away once more.

How am I going to marry him?

"Topolino, don't cry," my father says from his bed, his voice thick and gravelly.

I turn quickly and throw myself on the bed. "Father," I sob, so happy to see him awake. "Are you okay?" I press the button to call a nurse, and then take my father's hand in mine. "I thought you were going to die," I sob.

"It will take more than that to kill me off, Natalia. I've taken bullets and stabbings, and none of those things killed me. This never stood a chance," he says, kissing the top of my head.

The door opens and three nurses rush in, and I step back from the bed, letting them check him over. Alfonso comes in, his face hard and expressionless for a moment when he sees my father awake.

"Frank," he eventually says politely. He places the

coffees down on a table by the door and goes to my father. "You're okay," he says.

"Yes," my father replies, shooing the nurses away. "Who found me?" he asks immediately.

Alfonso's back goes stiff, and I watch as his jaw ticks in annoyance. "One of the Novello sons. Youngish kid. I called the ambulance for you and we've been here all night—isn't that right, Natalia?"

Frank and Alfonso both turn to look at me, their expressions serious.

"I believe it was another man that called the paramedics, if I'm not mistaken." I bite the inside of my cheek so I don't unleash the barrage of anger I feel toward Alfonso right now. He's lying, and worse, he's trying to get me to help him lie. "Wasn't it a friend of the Novellos that called them?"

Alfonso looks furious with me, and for the first time I'm actually fearful of him. What will our marriage be like? How will he punish me if I go against him once we are wed?

"The Novello brothers," my father says, his expression neutral. "Get them here, I want to talk to them."

"Talk to them?" Alfonso questions, his tone perplexed.

"Thank them personally for saving my life," my father adds.

Silence drops between us all—anger, resentment, jealousy. We're all adults here, and yet it feels like we're in a schoolyard.

"Of course, Frank. I'll get right on it for you." Alfonso turns to me, coming close. His furious gaze bores into mine and I force myself not to move as he leans in and kisses both of my cheeks. "Not long now, cara mia." And then he leaves.

My father watches from the bed, his expression still blank. He's not the sort of man to ever go back on his word or to change his mind. Once he makes a decision, he sticks with it. That's how he's achieved so much in life, from backyard gambling to million-dollar drug deals. My father knows people and he knows how to get the best from them.

"Where is your mother?" he asks, interrupting my thoughts.

I hesitate but realize that there's little point in lying to him. "I don't know," I finally answer honestly.

He sighs heavily. "Go home and get some sleep, Natalia. Check she's okay for me."

"I don't want to leave you." I move closer to his bed and sit down next to him, my eyes imploring not to send me away.

"I know, but your mother, she's fragile, delicate—she needs you right now. Go and make sure she is okay and then bring her back with you later. The doctors will be coming in soon, no doubt. There's nothing else you can do right now."

I nod and kiss his cheek. "I'll be back soon, I promise."

He cups my face in his large hands and stares at me. "My daughter, you have grown into such a beautiful woman. I hope you know that I only ever want the best for you. Wealth, security, respect. You deserve the world and the stars combined." He sighs and I notice real emotion on his face. "You are my one true love, daughter. Everything I do I do for you."

Tears prickle my eyes again. "Father?"

He kisses my cheeks once more. "Go, go find your mother, make sure she is okay."

I nod and leave, more confused than I've ever felt before.

When I return later that afternoon, I have my mother with me. She's barely sober, but she puts on a good show. It seems that even after the party finished last night, she continued drinking until the early morning.

We walk down the long corridor and I frown as I see several men in suits outside my father's room.

"I told you he was fine," my mother slurs. "Always working, even on his deathbed."

"Mother!" I snap, and she looks at me in shock because I never raise my voice. "He's not on his deathbed. He's going to be fine—not that you would know, since I've had to drag you here."

Her mouth opens and closes in shock before she finally pulls herself together. "You're right. He's the cat with nine lives. Nothing short of a miracle will finish that man off." She storms forward and I stare at her in shock.

I've always known my mother was unhappy, but this week is opening up so many wounds, it seems, and from those wounds, secrets are spilling free.

Donny, my father's head of security, is standing at the door with the men I met last night. I recognize them immediately; how could I not? All three were attractive. Tall, broad, wearing expensive suits. The one that had been flirting with me stands up straighter when he sees me, and I can't help the blush rising to my cheeks. There's no denying his attractiveness, or the wildness that simmers just below the surface. It intrigues me, pulling me in. My entire life has been sheltered, and I think this man would show me all the things I have been missing out on.

What am I thinking? I'm marrying Alfonso.

He reaches for my hand and kisses the back of it. "So good to see you again."

"I want to thank you all for helping my father last night," I say confidently as my mother walks straight into my father's room without sparing them a second glance. "I'm Natalia, Frank's daughter."

The more serious one's gaze is turned on me, and he

watches me acutely. I feel under inspection, like I'm under a microscope. My skin is tingling from his intense stare, but I try to ignore it. Try to not shiver under his scrutiny. The loose-fitting sweater I'm wearing doesn't keep away the heat that rises in me as his intensity burns brighter.

"Sisco." The first man kisses my hand again. "These are my brothers, Dominic and Joey."

I look at the other two, seeing the clear resemblance between the three now. Each has their own look about them. Sisco looks wild and untamed, a mischievous sparkle to his eye. He's handsome in a way that no doubt has women drawn to him like he's a magnet. Joey is younger than the other two, with a dimple in one cheek that pulls in further when he smiles. He too has a mischievous air about him. He looks good in a suit, and he's cocky and arrogant enough to know that. And then there's Dominic. He's dark and mysterious. He doesn't have the same quality as the other two. He seems burdened with dark thoughts—worries, perhaps. His eyes are intense, and when he reaches over and takes both my hands in his I realize how large they are compared to mine, swallowing them up in one. Dominic is larger than the other two men—not that they're small at all, but Dominic must have an intense workout schedule, because his suit is straining to contain him.

His jaw ticks as he watches me, and I feel the blush in my cheeks growing hotter. I squeeze my thighs together tightly as my body unwillingly responds to him.

"She had an evil face, smothered by hypocrisy, but her manners were excellent," Sisco says, drawing my attention back to him. He's grinning wildly and it sends a shiver down my spine.

"Excuse me?" I ask, confused, shocked, turned on.

Joey laughs. "Don't mind him." It's his turn to take my hand now, and he kisses the back of it, his lips staying there for a beat too long as he looks up at me through his dark lashes. It's a kiss on the hand, an action that has been done a thousand times in my life—my father commands respect for him and for his family from everyone—but this feels like more than that. This is the embodiment of seduction, and this time I can't refrain the tremble of excitement that runs through me.

The door to my father's room opens and Alfonso steps out, his expression turning dark when he sees me standing there, surrounded by these three men. My thighs squeezing together, my nipples hard, excitement flushing my cheeks. He reads me in seconds and he doesn't like the plot.

"Cara mia," he says sternly, a warning to them, and to me, "your father begs a moment of your time." He looks over at the Novello brothers, and Joey releases my hand after another kiss—which I'm more than certain was done to incite Alfonso's rage. "He also wishes to pay his respects to you." He's talking to all three of them, but he looks at Dominic.

Alfonso holds the door open and nods for me to enter, and I do, willing the heat in my cheeks to disappear. Mother is sitting by my father's bedside, looking almost bored as we all enter, though I see her expression perk up in interest when she sees the brothers behind me.

Father is looking better than earlier. He has a plastic tube in his hand that is attached to a bag of fluids next to his bed. But his color has returned to his face, which gives me hope. When we're all sitting or standing comfortably, he clears his throat.

"I want to thank you for what you did last night, Dominic. If it weren't for you, I'm not sure what would have happened." He hates admitting that. I can see it in his eyes how much it pains him to admit that he's human and not invincible. "I wanted to pay my respects to you and thank you in person."

Dominic moves closer and gives a nod of thanks. "If I may, it was my brother Joey who found you and began the CPR."

For some reason I admire Dominic for admitting this. It shows confidence and respect in himself and his brother. He isn't afraid of sharing the limelight with someone else. And he doesn't have to lie to prove his worth, unlike Alfonso.

My father's gaze moves to Joey and he nods his thanks. "I heard about your own father, Michael. It was a shock to us all. He was a good man. Strong within the community. I want you to know that I'm doing what I can to help you find

39

out who did it. I've uncovered a great many things since the funeral, but further digging is required. However, my resources are your resources."

"That's greatly appreciated, Mr. Costello," Dominic says. "We won't rest until we find the bastard who did this and destroy him and everything he holds dear."

His words make me shiver in fear, even though I clearly had nothing to do with his father's death. Dominic means business, and when I look at his brothers, I see the same deathly vengeance emanating from each of them.

"Please, call me Frank. Your father and I had a many business dealings over the years, but we tended to stick to our own areas," my father continues. "I'd like to change that and hope to strike up business with your family."

Dominic nods. "I think that would be good for both of our standings. I have many fresh ideas that my father and I were working on."

"I'd like to hear them, but perhaps when I'm not sitting with my ass out, huh?" He laughs and Dominic joins in.

His laugh is deep, a rumble coming from deep within his chest like a lion's roar. It makes me smile, and father glances in my direction when I do. We share a moment. A father daughter moment that no one can break. Finally, however, he looks back to Dominic.

"I'd like to repay you in some way, for last night," my father adds.

"That's not necessary," Dominic says, interrupting him.

My father holds up a hand. "It is." He turns to my mother, taking her hand and squeezing it tightly. "If it weren't for you, I'd be dead. My wife, my daughter . . ." He shakes his head, his emotions getting the better of him. "Who knows what would have happened to them. I'm not ready to leave this world just yet, and perhaps it's been arrogant of me not to put steps in place for their safety. I thought I was doing what was right, but there comes a time in a man's life when he recognizes that he has been wrong. That he must change for those that he loves."

I'm staring in shock, confused by the man in the bed. This isn't my father. This isn't the man who raised me to believe that you never show any weakness, any vulnerability, of any kind. Yet here he is, splaying his vulnerability to the world.

Maybe it's the drugs they have him on.

Or the lack of sleep.

Or the near-death experience.

It could be a hundred things, or none of them at all. All I know is that my father, the great Frank Costello, feared Don of the underworld, is as close to tears as I've ever seen him. Even my mother looks visibly shocked by his confession.

Alfonso throws me a sympathetic look and steps forward. "If I may, Frank," he says, his voice sickly smooth.

"No, you may not," my father snaps, his soft face turning

hard as steel as he stares Alfonso down.

"Frank," he begins, his features hardening like he's gearing for battle.

"Enough! I have heard enough from you." My father takes a deep breath, a hard scowl on his face.

Donny clears his throat, making Alfonso aware that he's getting close to crossing a line and that he'll step in if need be.

I'm even more confused now. Alfonso and my father have been as close as brothers for years, and now my father looks ready to turn on him. What is happening? Even Alfonso looks confused, and a scowl forms on his face.

My father turns his attention back to Dominic, a look of resolve set on his pale face. "Whatever you want. Whatever you need. No matter the price. Name it and it's yours."

The room is silent for several moments, the tension so thick you could scoop it with a spoon. I can tell Alfonso wants to say something but he's biting his tongue. He takes a step back, coming closer to me, his large frame pressing against my side and making me feel tiny and fragile next to him.

"You need some time to think about it, that's okay," my father continues, unperturbed by the atmosphere in the room. "Take some time. I have businesses, properties, a strong drug trade, half of the city's police force in my back pocket. Take the time you need and then get back to me with what you want, and it's yours. No questions asked." He picks up the glass of water from next to him. His hand shakes as he brings it to his mouth. He takes a long swallow, and for a moment all I see is a tired, frightened old man, nothing of the strong, take-no-shit man I've come to know and love. He puts the water back down. "But don't take too long," he snaps, trying to regain his composure. "My offer expires if you take too long."

"I already know what I want," Dominic says, his voice firm and commanding.

"Name it."

He holds my father's gaze, his hands in his pockets casually like he's not asking for anything of importance. "Natalia," he says, like he's ordering a Frappuccino from Starbucks.

"Yes?" I automatically reply, thinking that's he's asking me for something. Everyone, barring my father and Dominic, turns to look at me, and I'm confused for a moment before it hits me: He's not asking me for anything. He's asking my father for me.

My father's gaze moves to me, and I'm too in shock to say anything. To yell no. To yell yes. To argue the point that I'm his daughter and not an item to trade with. To yell that Alfonso was a bad choice, but at least I knew him. This man is a stranger. My own mother is staring in shock, confused as hell as to what is happening.

"Frank?" she stammers.

"I think it will be good for business. Combining our two families, bringing our businesses together. Or collective enforcement," Dominic adds casually.

"Fuck you!" Alfonso growls. "Natalia is not on the table to be traded."

"Well, I did say anything," father says with the quiet patience of a man making a serious decision. He strokes a hand over his chin, the drip attached to his hand banging lightly on the pole next to his bed.

I look over at Sisco and see that he's grinning from ear to ear, clearly more than happy about this turn of events. He glances between us all. His untamed gaze moving from me to my father, to his brothers and finally to Alfonso.

And then all hell breaks loose.

Alfonso pulls out his gun and aims it at Dominic, and then Joey and Sisco pull out their guns and aim them at Alfonso. I flinch at the sight of so many guns in such a small space, positive that someone, if not several men, are about to die, and I'm going to be a witness to it. Worryingly, Sisco and Joey look positively excited by the prospect of bloodshed.

"How dare you disrespect me like this!" Alfonso yells. "You know that the girl is promised to me."

Yet Dominic still stands there, his hands still in his pockets, his stature is like steel, commanding respect and authority. He's all business with no fucks to give as he holds my father's gaze, oblivious to—or just uncaring about—the gun aimed at his head. And he knows Alfonso, so he can't be stupid enough not to think that he won't blow his brains out without a second thought.

"Well?" Dominic prompts, ignoring the commotion behind him. "Do we have a deal, Frank?"

My father's gaze moves from me back to Dominic. He swallows thickly and holds out his hand. "Done," he says.

"Like hell," Alfonso roars angrily. "She's mine!" He grabs me by the wrist to prove his claim upon me, and I wince. His gun is still aimed at the back of Dominic's head, but Dominic hasn't even turned around and noticed.

"Let go of me," I whimper as his grip tightens on me.

Donny takes a step forward, but it's irrelevant because Sisco presses the barrel of his gun into Alfonso's head.

"You heard the lady," he growls, all amusement gone. And I suddenly see the darkness that was brimming under his skin earlier. He wants to shoot Alfonso. He delights in death and destruction. He's terrifying and mesmerizing all in one.

Alfonso side-eyes me, his nostrils flaring in fury. "Natalia, cara mia," he says through gritted teeth as he tries to keep his temper in check. "Tell them that you're mine."

"I said, let go of me," I say again, stronger this time.

His mouth purses into a thin line and he finally lets go

of my wrist. Joey gently pulls me to his chest. I go without argument because Alfonso looks like he might go on a killing spree at any moment, and by the hatred pouring from him, I would be his first victim.

"You're okay," Joey soothes, his strong arms wrapped around me, holding me to him.

I stay there, wrapped in his embrace, when I know I should shrug out from under his grip. But he smells so good—like cologne and soap. But mostly, I feel relief. Relief that I won't be marrying Alfonso, a man over twice my age who's stared at me like I was a piece of meat since I was just a young girl.

I peer out from under Joey's arm and watch as Dominic and my father shake hands.

Done.

I'm a done deal.

Traded off and passed around to the highest bidder.

I should be infuriated or devastated, and yet I don't feel anything of the sort. The only thing I feel is the rush of excitement.

Chapter 4

Dominic

All four of us are sitting in the limousine in silence. Sisco's knee is bouncing up and down, up and down, up and down. His gaze never leaving Natalia. Joey is leaning back, his arm slung over the back of her chair, a drink in his other hand. And Natalia. She's staring out the window in silence, like she's in a daze.

I like her, this one. Meek, amiable. Most mafia women are too damn headstrong for their own good, arguing back and demanding things. Natalia isn't like that. She knows how to take orders. How to bend to a man's whim. And better yet, she's pure, untouched. My dick twitches.

It's been like steel since I first saw her. And now she is mine. All mine . . . well, all ours. She'll need some time to adjust to that, I think, but I have no doubt that she'll fit right in.

"Where are we going?" she asks, her soft voice breaking the silence.

"Home," Joey drolls, taking another sip of his drink.

I watch her bite the inside of her cheek as she tries to hold back her annoyance with Joey's answer. She wanted more than that. A destination, a place of some sort. Of course, Joey knows this; he's just tempting her to speak again. Communication will be key to this transaction.

"You'll see," Sisco continues, leaning forward in his chair. He wrings his hands out in front of him, and I know he's refraining from touching her. "You'll like it."

"Don't worry, it's not some crazed sex dungeon. Our mom and sister live there too, so it's got a woman's touch, but you can add to it if you like," Joey says, watching her carefully.

"Oh," she says, her wide eyes moving over each one of us like we're lions in waiting, and then she returns to staring out the window.

Back at the mansion, I trail after Joey and Sisco as they lead Natalia to what will be her room. My hands are in my pockets casually, like I couldn't give a damn that she's here. She looks back at me over her shoulder every once in a while, like she's checking that I'm still there. My brothers are eager to show her various parts of the house and are oblivious to the fact that she's not really paying attention.

She's confused as to what's expected of her.

Who she belongs to.

What is required.

She'll understand soon enough, though.

"And this is your room," Sisco says, pushing open her bedroom door.

The room is warm and bright, the opposite of her mood. Sunlight streams in through the windows and splashes across the walls. I know she likes it as soon as she enters. It's big, with tall ceilings and huge sash windows that look out over our extensive grounds. The bed is vast, and handmade with ornate woodwork around the frame. The room has its own bathroom, with a large bath and walk-in shower.

"We've already got your things being packed up and sent here," Sisco continues.

Natalia turns and looks at him in puzzlement. "By whom?"

"Some angry French woman," Joey says with a laugh.

"Mary," Natalia says with a soft smile. "She was my nursemaid."

I'm leaning against the doorframe watching, my hands still in my pockets. She looks over at me, her smile dropping and a blush rising to her cheeks.

Sisco and Joey turn to look at me and then back to her.

"Don't mind him," Joey says. "He's the moody, mysterious one," he mocks.

"He tries to be moody and mysterious but we all know that he's just an asshole," Sisco joins in, and both of my idiotic brothers laugh.

Natalia starts to smirk but uses her hand to cover it. I wish she wouldn't do that. I like seeing her full lips turn up in a smile. I can imagine them wrapping around my . . .

"Ain't that right, brother?" Sisco says.

I push off the wall and give him the middle finger before walking away.

"Little sister," I say, rising from my chair. I catch Eva around the waist and spin her around.

"Dom!" She squeals with laughter as I set about tickling her. "Stop," she screams, laughing harder. "I'm gonna pee!"

I stop tickling her and release her. "I'd better stop then, huh? We can't have you peeing yourself."

Her cheeks are flushed and she bends over and picks up her school bag, which she'd thrown down upon seeing me. She settles herself in the large chair by the fireplace, watching as I settle in the one opposite. It was barely four months ago that this was our father and her sitting here, ready to discuss their day. I've done everything within my power to keep this routine for her.

"Well?" I ask, my fingertips peaked under my chin. "How was the test?"

She rolls her eyes and makes a gagging sound. "Awful, but I don't care."

"You should always care. Your education is important. A woman with no intelligence has nothing to offer the world."

"I might be a model," she taunts.

"How about a scientist," I suggest.

"How about a pop star?"

"A mathematician?"

"An actress?"

"You slay me, Eva," I say with feigned upset. "Can you not at least pretend to that you intend to use your brain for something?"

She rolls her eyes again. "Fine. An archaeologist."

I smirk at her. "A good choice. You'll see the world if nothing else."

Claire C Riley

"Who's the girl upstairs?" she asks, her legs swinging back and forth on the armchair.

My mouth quirks. For everything she has been through, Eva has bounced back so well. And she never misses anything.

"She's . . ." I pause, unsure how to phrase it without making Natalia sound cheap or me sound like a monster.

"Are you dating?"

I sigh. "Sort of."

"You like her though?"

"I suppose."

"And Sisco?"

"He likes her too."

"And Joey?" she says, her expression serious, as any child's would be while they tried to untangle the messy lives of grownups.

I nod and a small frown puckers between her eyes.

"It's complicated," I stress. But it's not—not really. Not for me.

"So, you all like her?" she asks.

I nod.

"And does she like you?"

"She's safe with us," I say instead of answering the question. I know she likes Sisco; I've seen the way her chest rises and falls when he gets that wild look about him. She admires his daring, his craziness. And her cheeks flush when she's near Joey. She likes that he makes her feel young and reckless, like a twenty-year-old should. And me—there's no denying the way her pupils dilate when she's near me.

Yes, she likes us all. Though she may not realize the consequence of that yet. But she will.

Eva pats my knee. "She looks kind. I think she'll fit right in with us."

I nod in agreement. "I think so too."

She scoots off the edge of her chair. "I need to go do my homework. Is Mom in her room?"

I nod and Eva leaves. I watch as she clicks my office door closed. I'm not sure Eva truly understands what's happening, or who Natalia is to us now, but she's smart enough to make her own mind up about it.

And she's right, Natalia is kind, so I have no worries that she won't fit in here.

Eventually.

Chapter 5

Natalia

After dressing in a short black embellished dress, I make my way down to the waiting limousine. Sisco and Joey have barely left my side since I arrived here, but I insisted I be left to dress on my own. All three men are at the bottom of the stairs now, and they turn to stare. Wearing thousand-dollar suits and with their hair slicked back, you'd mistake them for models, and I swallow, wishing I'd chosen the longer dress. The urge to squeeze my thighs together at the sight of them is enough to drive me to distraction.

Sisco whistles as I make it to the bottom step and he takes an arm as Joey takes my other. Dominic looks me up and down approvingly before turning on his heel and heading to the limousine, and I try not to be hurt by his uninterested reaction to me.

I don't really understand my place here yet, but I was supposed to marry Alfonso until Dominic asked for me. Therefore, I can only think that I'm supposed to be Dominic's wife-to-be now. Yet he's barely said a handful of words to me. At least his brothers have been attentive, and I can't deny that I enjoy their attention.

"You like steak?" Sisco asks as the car heads down the long driveway. "I love steak. Gotta be rare, pepper sauce." He licks his lips and it's ridiculous how sensual such a simple act is. "I like fries and salsa too. I make a mean homemade salsa. I'll make it for you sometime. You'll love it, especially if you like chili..."

Joey chuckles and Sisco stops talking and looks over at him sharply. "Give her some space, brother."

"I prefer well-baked cannelloni, but steak is good too, I guess," I smart.

Sisco laughs like I'm the most hilarious woman ever, and I grin. Joey has his arm slung over the back of my seat again, and one of his fingers is stroking along the top of my shoulders. It's such a small movement that I shouldn't even notice it, really, but as with all these men, I can't help but be hyper-aware of everything they do. Every movement, every laugh, every smile, every touch is turning me to molten fire.

"I'm going to get you the best steak you've ever had in

your life, Natalia," Sisco promises.

I let my gaze slide to Dominic as Sisco talks, noticing that he's watching me intently, that dark look back on his face. He looks almost angry, but I know I haven't done anything to anger him.

I'm terrified and turned on, and I don't know what to do with these feelings. I'm still horrified that my father basically sold me off to Dominic, and yet I can't be too angry because I'd rather it be Dominic than Alfonso. At least we're closer in age. At least Dominic hasn't watched me grow from baby to toddler to teenager to woman. There was something almost perverted in the way Alfonso wanted me for his wife.

So no, I can't be truly angry—only shocked.

And I can't be too shocked, either, because a part of me that I didn't know even existed until yesterday is whispering bad things in my ear. I want Dominic to talk to me. To shower me with attention the way Joey and Sisco do.

We pull up to the restaurant and Sisco holds the door open for me. He takes one arm and Joey takes the other, while Dominic walks ahead of us. I'm hyper-aware of everyone's gaze on us as we walk inside and take a seat in the VIP area. I know it must look bad—one woman with three men—but it's not like that, and they need to mind their own business or I have no doubt that one of the brothers will make these people regret their perverted thoughts.

"Drink, madame?" the waiter asks, but before I can

answer Dominic orders two bottles of red wine for the table. Each bottle is easily two hundred dollars, and even though I know that I should be grateful, I can't help but scowl at him.

All my life men have ordered me around and told me what I could and couldn't do. It shouldn't bother me; I should be used to it by now—and yet I feel bolder with the Novello brothers. Something about being with them gives me strength.

"You don't approve, Natalia?" Dominic asks with dark amusement, pulling me away from my irritated thoughts.

"Red is fine," I say, holding his gaze. The corner of his mouth quirks up and I know that I've pleased him. I like that look on him. The dark threads of thrill dance across my skin, so I decide to push my luck that little bit more. "But I'd love a bourbon."

The air is thick as he assesses me, holding my gaze steady. Sisco and Joey are quiet as they watch how it is all unfolding, and I'm just about to tell him to forget about it when he looks up at the waiter.

"You heard the lady." He waves his hand and the waiter leaves.

I think we're finally getting somewhere, but instead of talking to me he pulls out his cell phone and starts tapping away at the screen. The waiter returns with the wine and the bourbon and takes our orders. Dominic orders his steak and then looks over at me.

"I presume you'd like to order for yourself again, Natalia?" He steeples his fingers beneath his chin and I can't decide if I've angered him or if he's amused, so I choose to go with it.

I order my food and the waiter leaves, and I drink my bourbon in barely three sips because I'm so nervous. We're still receiving looks from other people, and I know I'm being paranoid but I can't stop my cheeks from growing hot under everyone's stares.

Joey's hand slides over my knee under the table and I stare at him in shock. He's talking to Sisco, though, and not even looking at me, as if the act is so casual he isn't even thinking about it.

"I need to go to the bathroom," I say, and excuse myself.

I feel everyone's eyes on me as I leave the main room and head to the bathroom, willing my knees not to knock as I walk.

I'm scared.

I'm nervous.

I'm excited.

I'm convinced I've done something wrong because Dominic won't come near me, and yet I can't think what it could be. In the bathroom I powder my nose and will myself to calm the hell down. My stomach is fluttering with nerves. I head into a stall and I'm about to flush the toilet when I hear voices.

"Did you see her?"

"She's beautiful, but I mean, it's all fake, right?"

"Right."

"Tits, lips, I heard even her ass is fake," the other woman cackles.

I don't know why, but I stay frozen to the spot, listening. They can't be talking about me, and yet something tells me that they are. My mother always told me that what someone says about you is more about them, and yet it still hurts. I don't even know these women.

"And such a slut. Three men, what is that all about?"

"I heard her daddy sold her to them—a bad business deal gone wrong or something."

"I wouldn't mind being sold to them."

They both laugh.

"Princess or not, she's just like the rest of us."

"Worse," the other one agrees, and they both leave.

I feel like I'm on fire. Shame and humiliation are burning like an inferno inside me, and I can't stop shaking. People think I've been sold to them—all of them! I'll never live this down. The shame will follow me forever. And what will my father say when he finds out? He'll kill them, and then me, for sure.

I thought they'd saved me, but they've ruined me forever.

I leave the bathroom, intent on getting the hell out of there and away from them. I have no idea where to go, though. I can't go home, and I don't have any friends. I just need to go, though. I can't walk back in there and see all those faces staring at me, all thinking the same thing.

My heels click noisily over the marble floor of the foyer, and I'm almost at the door when I hear him call my name.

"Natalia?"

Dominic's voice is behind me and I pause momentarily, his voice commanding me to stop. But then I grit my teeth and ignore him. I keep on walking, my steps growing quicker as I speed away from him and this place of humiliation.

The night is cool and I wrap my arms around my bare shoulders, wishing that I'd thought to bring my jacket with me. Night has fallen, and with it the temperature has dropped, but embarrassment is still burning inside me, and now that I'm out of there I can't stop the tears from falling either.

I'm so confused and so lost and I have nowhere to go, no one I can trust, barring Mary, but I can't bring her into this. I sit on the edge of the sidewalk and put my head in my hands and sob. Each tear is a bitter relief as I shed myself of the heavy burden. Each shudder of grief makes me even more confused than the last until, in the end, I don't even know why I'm crying.

I couldn't give a damn what those people think of me. If they had any sense about them, they wouldn't speak about me like that because I know far too many powerful men. I look up at the sound of a car coming to a stop and watch as the door to Dominic's limousine opens.

"Get in," he orders, his face shrouded in darkness.

I ignore him, my nipples hardening when he leans forward, his blue eyes piercing me from the darkness.

"Natalia," he warns, "don't make me ask twice or there'll be hell to pay."

I bite the inside of my cheek and squeeze my thighs together. "Go away."

A rumble comes from his chest and he sits back. Sisco climbs out of the limo and stands in front of me, his hand held out. I stubbornly refuse to take it at first, so he drops to his haunches and looks at me giving a heavy sigh.

"Hey, beautiful."

I look at him, wincing as he raises a hand and I think he's going to slap me, but instead he runs his thumb under my eyes and wipes away my tears before licking them from his thumb. His nostrils flare like my sadness turns him on.

"Come on," he says, and this time I take his hand and let him lead me to the car.

We slide in, me sitting between Sisco and Joey and, as usual, Dominic sitting opposite us, a glass in one hand. The tension is suffocating and I begin to panic that I shouldn't have trusted Sisco. That I should have run away when he offered me his hand. Dominic scares me, but this silence is even more frightening than his dark mood. Are they going to kill me? I've offended him, and princess or not, he could make me disappear. My father is weak right now; no one is scared of him. Frank Costello, the mafia don of NYC, had a heart attack; he's on his last legs and his businesses are going to be swept up from beneath him. I know that's why my father agreed to Dominic's wishes. Combining the two families makes them both strong.

"Why did you leave?" he asks, his voice stern, his tone dark.

Joey's hand is stroking my back again, and Sisco's thigh is pressed up against mine. My chest feels tight, and the words won't come.

"Natalia." Dominic says my name again, a warning on his lips. "Answer me."

Sisco leans in and kisses my neck and I shudder. Joey's hand strays to my knee, his thumb now stroking the sensitive bare skin. My chest feels hot and I look between them both, confusion and desire flaring equally.

"I heard what people were saying," I stutter, breathless.

"And what were they saying?" Dominic asks.

I'm breathing hard, my chest rising and falling heavily. I look right at Dominic, refusing to show him how scared I am of him.

"They assumed I was sleeping with all three of you. That you had bought me from my father because of a deal gone bad," I say, the words sounding bitter and angry.

Dominic takes a sip from the drink in his hand. "I didn't buy you, Natalia," he says. "I've never needed to buy a woman in my life," he chuckles.

The arrogance of his statement angers me and I narrow my eyes. I decide to ask the question that's been on my mind since I arrived at their home. "Why won't you come near me?"

His mouth twitches in amusement. Joey's stroking has moved higher, and Sisco has taken to stroking the other knee. Every nerve is on fire. Everything heightened to unbelievable limits.

"So, you want me to come near you, little mouse?" he asks, one eyebrow rising like he's daring me.

"That's not what I said," I argue.

"Isn't it?"

I roll my eyes and look away. I need to get the hell out of here. I don't know what's going on, but I can't think with Sisco and Joey's hands on me and Dominic sitting there watching, talking in riddles.

"Natalia, if you want me to touch you, all you have to do was ask," he says, a playfulness in his tone.

"I'm not a whore, Dominic," I snap, surprised by my own temper.

He smiles, reaching down to unbutton his suit jacket. He leans forwards, his expression impassive. "Natalia, I wouldn't have wanted you if you were a whore. It's your purity and innocence I wanted."

I don't know what to say to that. My thoughts are becoming muddled. I don't know what he wants from me. I don't understand what's happening here. My skin feels hot, but Joey's touch is hotter. Sisco's kisses on the sensitive skin at my neck are igniting me, and I take a shuddering breath like all the air is being sucked out of the car.

Dominic and I stare at one another, neither one of us willing to back down. Joey and Sisco's hands have gone up even higher on my thighs, and before I can stop them, Sisco has pushed my skirt up and Joey's hands are on my knees pushing my legs firmly apart. My legs spread and I yelp in shock.

"What are you..." I'm about to tell them to get the hell off me, but then Joey's hand is pushing my panties to one side and pressing his thick fingers against my wet entrance and I gasp in shock. I'm embarrassed by how wet I am, my core pulsing with need.

My hands curl into small fists. I need to push his hand away but I refuse to back down from Dominic, to give him this power to Lord over me. I try to close my legs, but Sisco gently pushes them back apart.

"It's okay, beautiful," he murmurs against my neck, his breath hot against my skin.

And it is okay.

It feels good.

So good.

And then Joey's fingers are pushing inside of me and I'm gasping again, my own hands clawing at Sisco and Joey's thighs on either side of me. Joey strums me, setting my body on fire, and I buck automatically against his hand with a long groan.

My cheeks are flaming red with desire and embarrassment as Joey fucks me with his fingers and Sisco kisses my neck. His tongue moves over my skin, making me groan again. And still Dominic sits back and watches with unfaltering calm, refusing to look away, and so of course, I also won't look away either. I refuse to let him think he has the power here, that he controls me. And if he won't touch me and take me for himself, perhaps this will convince him to.

Perhaps... a soft moan escapes my lips as Joey slips another finger inside me. I'm riding a wave of desire, getting lost in the movements of Joey's fingers as he stretches me wider. I should be embarrassed but for some reason I'm not. Right now, I don't care about anything but the feel of these men's hands on my skin and the intense look on Dominic's face as he watches them touching me. It's too dark to see if he's hard but I realize as soon as the thought enters my head that I want him to be. I want him to be turned on by this—by me.

His jaw ticks and he lifts his glass to his mouth and takes another calm sip. I want to kiss him, I realize. I want to taste the whiskey on his lips and suck it from his tongue. I moan loudly, my head tilting to one side to allow Sisco better access to my throat. His hands move down the front of my dress, pushing it down to reveal my heaving chest.

What is happening to me? This isn't me, my mind screams, but I don't stop either one of them. I don't want them to stop. I want more.

I'm supposed to be demure. Fragile. Weak. Just like my mother. To do as I'm told and ask no questions. I'm supposed to give pleasure and forgo my own, and yet here these men are giving me pleasure and asking for nothing in return.

Will I be punished, I wonder idly, before deciding I don't care.

Joey hooks his fingers, hitting just the right spot to make my insides tremble.

"Oh god," I whimper as a wave begins to build inside me, my core tightening.

"Natalia." Dominic says my name firmly. A warning? A threat? A promise? "Tell me."

Tell him?

Tell him what?

I stare at him, confused, desire flooding my brazen body. His grip is tight around his glass, his tattooed knuckles white. His jaw is ticking, and he swallows, his gaze never leaving mine.

He's begging, I realize.

He wants me.

I stare at him in confusion, his eyes hooded and his lips parted. He puts down his drink and sits forward in his seat again, his beautiful blue eyes still locked on mine. Sisco has parted my legs further. He drops to his knees between them and I'm torn between telling him to stop and allowing this to continue. In the end, it's the way Dominic's nostrils flare that force me to sit back and allow Sisco to do as he pleases. He pulls my panties down my quivering thighs with the expertise of someone who has done this a thousand times before.

"Tell me that you want me to touch you, little mouse," Dominic demands, his nostrils flaring.

And despite the words being on the tip of my tongue, I clamp my jaw shut and refuse to give him what he wants. If he wants any part of me, he'll ask for it. Or take it. But I refuse to beg him to touch me.

Joey strums me to perfection and Sisco latches his mouth onto my pussy and I call out loudly—too loudly. It's undistinguishable what I say—even I don't know. Dominic holds me prisoner with his gaze while his brothers pleasure my body. I slam a hand up to the ceiling of the Limousine as Sisco's tongue swirls around my clit and I buck against his mouth, a soft moan escaping my lips. Joey slides his fingers out, parting my lips, and Sisco slides his tongue up the full length of me and then back down.

He parts me with his tongue, the heat of his mouth

making pleasure unfurl inside of me. The wave that has been building comes crashing down, drowning me, and I can't hold on to Dominic anymore. I release his gaze and close my eyes, throwing my head back as I ride the wave. Sisco's tongue slides up me again and Joey's thumb presses against my clit, wringing out every ounce of pleasure from my body.

I'm gasping.

I'm on fire.

I'm calling out and begging for something that I don't even know, my hands clawing at the expensive leather seats as I ride the wave of euphoria.

I feel parts of me; the innocent, obedient daughter of Frank Costello, falling away piece by piece. Crumbling into dust, and I know I will never be the same after this.

Chapter 6

Dominic

"**W**hy didn't you tell us?" Sisco roars, his anger echoing off the walls of our father's study. He grabs a glass and throws it against the wall. It shatters, scattering the floor with glass.

"I think you just answered your own question there, brother," Joey says, surprising me.

I quirk an eyebrow at him in agreement and he gives me a one-shoulder shrug.

"You should have told us. We should have been able to reap our own vengeance, Dom."

"I'm not disputing that," I say calmly.

"I would have made that bastard pay for months. I would have wrung every drop of blood from his fucking body. Strung him up by his intestines and made him eat them while he was still alive, and then . . ."

"Brother!" I bark, and he stops pacing and stares at me, hatred burning in his eyes. "That is exactly why I didn't tell you. I wanted it done. He paid a heavy price—believe me, he did. I didn't spare him any suffering. But I needed him out of the way. I didn't want word getting back to that fucking string-puller that we were on to him." I stop and glare at Sisco, my anger for Romy and his accomplice growing with every breath. "Brother, I didn't want him to have any warning that we were coming for him."

Sisco clenches and unclenches his hands into fists at his sides, his anger not backing down even though he knows I'm talking sense. I love my brothers, dearly, and I would do anything for them, but Sisco is a different man from most. He has no off switch. In some ways he's like a machine in the way he works; he sees something and he seeks it. Whether it be death or fucking, he gets what he wants.

"I swear to you, brother, when the time comes you can extract your revenge however you choose. This I promise." I say the words with every ounce of my being, hoping he'll be satisfied by my answer.

Joey walks to him, placing a heavy hand on his shoulder. He's the only one that can ever talk sense into him when he's like this, and I'm hoping he can do so now.

"Brother, I don't agree with the way Dom did this, but he is right. You and I both know it. He has all of our best interests at heart, and now we're one step closer to finding out the real culprit," Joey soothes.

"And that death you can take as long as you wish over," I agree.

Sisco's jaw is ticking, but he's coming back down. Thank fuck.

I perhaps shouldn't have told them about Romy just yet, but I hated the lie being there between us all. Nothing has ever come between my brothers and me, and with me heading the empire I didn't want the death of Romy, my father's executioner, to be the one thing that did.

I go to Sisco, standing in front of him, my gaze imploring him not to lose his shit and hate me for what I did. I've never begged for anything in my life, but I'd beg for his forgiveness in a heartbeat. There is no greater bond than that between my brothers and me.

"Big brother, I apologize. I thought I was doing the best for us."

Sisco watches me for a long moment, his anger draining from him before he reaches over and pulls me to his chest. He slaps my back heartily and hugs me tightly, our thousand-dollar suits creasing in brotherly love. When he pulls away, I know I'm forgiven.

"So, what now?" he asks.

What now indeed. I'm waiting for the bastard who set all of this in motion to make his next play, but so far he hasn't come out of his hole for his cut of meat. It can only be a matter of time though.

"We wait. He'll come for us, and we'll be ready," I say.

"Is that wise?" Joey asks, running his hands through his hair, his face anxious. "What about Mom and Eva?"

"What about Natalia?" Sisco adds.

I unbutton my jacket and perch myself on the edge of my father's desk. "We can protect them."

Joey and Sisco look between themselves and then back to me. I already know what they're thinking and I agree wholeheartedly. Natalia has no idea the pivotal role she plays in all of this, the power play I put in place by demanding her as our payment.

She's my smartest move yet and possibly my biggest mistake.

But how was I supposed to know that we would all fall so hard for her? Natalia Costello, the beautiful, untouched mafia princess of Frank Costello. The promised bride for Alfonso Rosso.

She is everything I ever dreamt of and more. Pliant to us all but still with fire in her eyes and willing to stand up to me. She's driving me crazy. I can only imagine the goddess she'll be once she discovers how powerful she is. My dick goes hard at the memory of her in the limousine. Her legs spread wide, my brothers' hands on her sweet pussy, and her gaze defiantly on mine as she came. I must grin or show in some way that I'm thinking about her, because my brothers laugh.

"She tasted good, brother. You're missing out," Sisco says, a grin in his tone.

"Yes, and so wet for us both," Joey adds, and they laugh again.

"Fuck you both. It was me she wanted," I grumble. But we all know that's a lie. She loved all of us on her, in her, watching her. She wanted all three of us. And she'll have us all, soon. But not until she begs for me. This is a lesson I'll make her learn.

I've never backed down from anything in my life, and I don't intend to now. I don't care how long it takes, or how many times I have to watch her cum on my brothers' tongue and fingers; until she begs me to take her, I won't touch her. It's a battle of wills now, and one I am more than willing to let play out.

Natalia is an unexpected advantage in all this mess, but one I am more than happy about.

"We need to get back to business," I say, closing the subject on Natalia for the moment, because I can't think straight when she is on my mind. She consumes me in a way that I've never felt before. I don't love the woman—I've never loved a woman in my life, other than my mom and

Eva—but I feel something for her. Something unexpected.

"So, tell me," I say, "how is business going?"

Things had been in a bad way before our father was murdered. From the outside, business was booming, but going legit is hard. Harder than we knew. And when our father had started handing his empire over to us, that was the route we'd wanted to take. I say legit, but there's only so legit men like us can go. Murder and death are in our veins, but there are certain things we could eliminate. Of course, this is what had pissed off so many people, and no doubt gotten our father killed.

I bore the brunt of that guilt on my shoulders, despite it being a joint decision.

Joey sighs. "We've finally cut all ties with the Russians."

He stalks over to the window and looks out. He didn't agree with this—going legit. He never completely wanted it, but he went along with it because he trusted us—Sisco and me—and he believed in what we were trying to build. The new direction we were going. While our bank balances grew from the blood money we collected, our sister and mother were in danger. I refused to do that any longer.

"They took it as expected, I presume?" I probe. I sound cold and heartless, but it cuts me when he speaks and tells me what I already know.

He's silent a beat before turning to look at me, his face expressionless. "We lost several men in the fallout."

I nod, the guilt ever-growing. "Make sure their families are well subsidized."

Money—it's the beginning and the end of everything.

"Do you think there will be more?" Sisco asks, going to stand with Joey. He places a heavy hand on his shoulder.

"Without a doubt," Joey says with a humorless laugh.

We're all silent, all thinking of the deaths on our hands from trying to go straight. To protect our family, we must destroy another's. Nothing about that sits well with my brothers or me, but no matter the guilt, my loyalty has to be with my own blood.

"Then we'll be ready for them too," I say, and go to stand with my brothers. I place a hand on their shoulders, looking between the two of them. "I know that this is hard. Believe me, I know, but we must protect our family. We can't protect them if we're dead."

Sisco laughs. "What makes you think we're going to die, brother?"

I smile at his confidence. "Frank Costello almost died yesterday," I say seriously. "His business was already being torn to shreds before he was in the ground, his wife and daughter in danger. I won't have that for our mother and Eva. All this has done is prove to me that this is the right decision for us. Everything I do, I do for them—and you, of course."

"Good and evil are so close as to be chained together in

the soul," Sisco quotes seriously.

"Indeed, dear brother," I agree.

Chapter 7

Natalia

When I wake, I wake to the sun on my face and the sound of birds outside my window. I stretch and smile, welcoming the day until I remember where I am and then the mortification of the night before hits me. Images of Joey's hand and Sisco's mouth between my legs in the limousine make my cheeks blush and I fling an arm over my face in embarrassment.

How am I going to face them all today?

How am I going to apologize to Dominic for what I let his brothers do to me?

Would he be angry with me?

With them?

I groan and roll over, facing the window, my eyes falling

on a young girl of no more than ten sitting and drawing in a sketchpad in the chair by the window. Her auburn hair is in a short bob around her face and she tucks it behind her ears as she swings her legs.

"Hello?" I say, sitting up with surprise, my hair tumbling around my shoulders.

She turns to me, and I know immediately that she must be the sister that I had been told about. There's no denying the relation to them. She has the same dimple as Joey, the same blue eyes as Dominic, and the same mischievous grin as Sisco.

"Hi." She waves. "I'm Eva. You're pretty."

I hold the covers to my chest, realizing that I'm wearing only my underwear. My cheeks flame again at the realization that someone must have undressed me because I have no recollection of getting undressed. I can't even remember arriving back at the mansion last night. After an orgasm that sent my pulse racing, I passed out in Sisco's arms.

That's the last thing I remember.

Mortification rolls through me.

"Thank you," I say, tucking my hair behind my ears. "I'm Natalia."

Eva smiles. "I know, you're my brother's girlfriend."

My heart skips a beat and I wonder which brother she's referring to, because even I don't know myself. I'm about to ask her who she thinks is my boyfriend when she jumps down from the chair and comes over to me with her pad and pencil.

"I drew you," she says proudly, showing me the drawing. It's actually pretty impressive for a ten-year-old.

"Wow, that's very good, Eva." I smile at her and her own smile grows bigger under my praise. "I should probably get dressed."

She picks up her pad, her smile falling when she hears a cry coming from somewhere else in the house.

"I better go," she says, rushing toward the door.

"Wait, what is that?"

It sounds pained, like an animal in distress.

"That's my mom," Eva says. She looks torn between wanting to stay and talk to me and wanting to go to her mom.

I look around the room, spotting a silk robe on the back of a chair, and decide to make a run for it. I slide on the robe and tie it tightly around my waist and go to her, holding out my hand.

"Do you want me to come with you, Eva?" I ask, my voice strong despite the screams growing louder.

She nods and takes my hand. Her large blue eyes staring up at me angelically. "Yes, please."

She pulls me out the door and we head down the long hallway. Every step makes my knees knock as the screaming and wailing increases, but Eva seems pretty calm. Surely it can't be so bad if she's willing to go toward the noises, I tell myself.

The crying suddenly stops just as we pull up outside a wooden door, and I look to Eva nervously. I'm the grownup here, so I know I need to suck it up and keep calm, but that's easier said than done. I push Eva a little behind me and crouch down to her.

"I'll go first. If it's not safe then you need to run and find your brothers, okay?" I say seriously.

She peers into my face with a mixture of confusion and what can only be described as adoration on her little face before she throws her arms around my shoulders and hugs me tightly. I'm speechless and in shock but I hug her back, feeling stronger and more confident. When she pulls out, she smiles at me.

"They've gone out," she says.

"Oh, well then, just run and hide somewhere. Do you have somewhere safe you can hide?" I ask.

She nods. "Yes, there's the old servants' hatch. I've hidden in there plenty of times. But it's okay, it's just my mom."

"Your mom?"

"Yeah. She's not well. I'll show you, come on. She'll like you, I just know it."

Eva pushes on the handle and the door opens inward, and then she pulls me in with her.

The room is much like mine, but it's messier, with clothes and makeup thrown everywhere. The bed is unmade, and it doesn't smell like anyone has cleaned in here for a long time. I don't see anyone at first, and then a woman comes out of the bathroom, her long, flowing robe billowing behind her.

"Mom," Eva says, still full of confidence, and yet she's holding onto my hand tightly so I wonder if it's all a show.

I see the blue eyes of Dominic staring back at me as the woman spins to look at us, her face spiraling through various emotions before settling on happiness.

"My little one," she says to Eva and opens her arms wide.

Eva releases my hand and runs to her, and they hug for a good long minute in silence.

I feel awkward and want to back out of the room and give them some space, but I also don't want to move in case I disturb them. It seems like they haven't seen each other in a really long time.

Eventually the woman lets go of Eva and notices me standing there. She looks me up and down, assessing me from head to foot and making me feel incredibly uncomfortable standing there in only a robe.

Eva looks to me and then back to her mom. "It's okay, Mom, this is Natalia."

Her expression is full of anxiety now, sadness creeping

into the edges of her short-lived happiness.

"You must be Eva's mom. She's told me so much about you," I say, in the hopes of winning her over, because she looks like she's going to flip out at any moment. "You're just as beautiful as she described."

The woman looks uncertain and then my compliment does what it always does to unstable women in power . . .

Eva's mom smiles and relaxes. She turns, forgetting Eva is there as she assesses herself in the mirror.

"Eva, sweetheart, could you fix my hair?" she coos, and Eva nods.

"Of course, Mom."

I watch as she picks up the hairbrush and begins to brush the knotty tangles, every tug making her more and more nervous.

I walk forward. "May I?" I ask, watching her mom in the mirror staring back at me. "It looks so soft," I coo with a smile.

Her mom nods and Eva hands me the brush, and then I spend the next ten minutes gently brushing her hair free of tangles.

"I can never find anything to wear," her mom complains, her beautiful blue eyes staring at me beseechingly. "I can never find anything in all this mess."

I nod encouragingly. "Let me help you tidy and then we can find something pretty for you to put on."

She smiles at me, her gaze straying to Eva, who's now sitting on the bed, sketching again. "She thinks I'm mad," she confides. "It's because of what they did to me."

My heart freezes in my chest and my hands stop working, a thousand and one awful thoughts moving through my mind.

Eva's mom reaches back and takes my hand, guiding it toward the right side of her head. She presses my fingertips to her skull and I feel a small dent.

"The bullet just missed the really important stuff," Eva says from the bed.

"But it got some of the important stuff, Eva!" her mom snaps. "Sometimes it hurts to think." Her face grows pained, creases between her eyebrows growing deeper. "I can't remember what I was doing and then it just hurts when I try to remember."

This house is filled with so much pain and anguish and all I can think of doing is hugging her, so I do. I reach down and wrap my arms around Eva's mom and hug her. It's awkward, the position not right, not to mention that I don't even know this woman. She pats my arm gently and starts to hum.

"I need something nice to wear for Michael tonight," she says. "He's going to take me out dancing."

I bite my lip so I don't cry, and then I stand up. "I'll help you pick out something really pretty." I finish brushing her hair and put the hairbrush down and she yawns. "Why don't you take a nap and I'll hang something up, ready for when you wake up," I say.

She nods and Eva scoots off the bed, allowing her mom to climb in. We pull the covers over her and she settles into sleep almost immediately. Eva and I pick up the clothes from the floor, carefully deciding what's clean and what's not, before dropping it in the hamper or hanging it in the large walk-in wardrobe. It takes us twenty minutes or so, and Eva's mom sleeps through it all. Every time I look up Eva is watching me, her piercing blue eyes examining my every move.

When we're done, I take her hand and smile at her. "We should probably get dressed, right?"

"Do you like pancakes?" Eva asks and I nod. She smiles wider. "I love pancakes with syrup and strawberries and cream, and..."

"We can go make some if you like," I offer.

If it's possible, Eva's smile grows even bigger, and I can't help but smile back. She's adorable in every way, and I find myself lost in my feelings for her. Already knowing that I'd do everything in my power to keep her safe.

I turn, squealing in fright when I see Dominic standing in the doorway watching us both. His expression is serious, a small furrow between his brows like he's trying to work something out. Like he's trying to work me out.

Eva smiles and runs to him, throwing her arms around him, and he smiles the most genuine smile I've ever seen on a man.

I make myself busy by picking out a beautiful dress for when their mother wakes up—though I suspect she won't remember the conversation when she wakes.

We all head out the door and I close it quietly behind me. He kisses her cheek and puts her down.

"Go and play for a little while, Eva. I need to talk to Natalia alone," he says.

Eva hugs me and runs back down the hallway. I turn to Dominic, noticing that he's watching me intently again.

"Let me walk you to your room, Natalia." He starts to walk and I sheepishly follow him.

I wonder, the entire time we walk, if he's going to yell at me. For last night with his brothers, for today with his mother, for speaking to his little sister. Or maybe for walking out of the restaurant last night. My heart is beating so heavily in my chest that I'm surprised he can't hear it. I don't know what the protocol is here, but I need him to know that I'll learn. That I'll do what's needed of me. I'm startled by my own thoughts. My own eager subservience to this man.

When we reach my room, he turns the handle and opens the door, pushing it open so I can enter first. Only, as I enter and go to pass him he wraps one hand around my throat and the other around my waist. I should scream or kick and fight him, but I don't. All I can do is lean back into him, submissive to his touch. My body automatically responds to him—his scent, his touch, his low growl down my ear.

"You smell so good, Natalia," he says, his breathy words caressing my throat, "I wonder what you'll taste like." His tongue darts out and slides up my throat towards my earlobe

I gasp at his words, automatically pushing myself back on him. I feel him hardening against my backside and I grind against him, wanting him, needing him. There's an itch I can't scratch, and I know he'll be able to reach it for me.

"Please," I beg as his grip on me tightens.

"Please what, Natalia? Say it and I'm yours." He kisses along my throat, sucking my earlobe into his mouth.

I want him more than I've ever wanted anything in my life. Seeing his mom like that, meeting his sweet sister, only made me want him more. It humanized the monster, and despite the fear I have of him, there's also a dark thrill of him wanting me so much.

"Say it," he growls, his cock pressed between my ass cheeks, eager and waiting.

My head is rolled back against his shoulder and I open my eyes, seeing his intense blue ones boring into me. Just waiting for the words to spill from my lips so that he can fuck me.

"No," I whimper. "Not yet."

He releases me immediately and I take a step away from him with a gasp.

"Well then, it seems we're at an impasse because I won't touch you until you beg me," he says, his words caressing my throat, "but don't think that I don't want you. That I don't think about you at night. That I don't imagine what it will feel like to fill that tight pussy of yours."

When I turn to look at him, I see a smile upon his face and I know I've pleased him. I don't know why it's so important, but I want to please him. Knowing I have makes me smile.

He takes a step forward, his hard body next to mine, and he peers down into my face. His hand reaches down, his fingers gripping the point of my chin gently and he tips my face up to his. "I'm going to fuck that smile off your beautiful face one day, Natalia. You won't walk straight for a week."

My smile falters—not through fear, but through heady desire.

"That thought pleases you," he taunts me, his gravelly voice slides over the soft curves of my body and I shudder. "We'll see how pleased you'll be when your throat is sore from screaming my name, princess."

I want to drop to my knees in front of him. I want to undo my robe and spread myself naked for him. I want his hands on me, in me. I want him to ravish every part of me. I can't think straight with him so close, and I wonder if there's something wrong with me. Because how can I be so turned on by such a threat? And yet I am.

We're nose to nose, heat burning between us. His hand leaves my chin and reaches up to wrap around my throat again. I keep my gaze on his, refusing to look away first.

"Defiant little thing aren't you," he taunts darkly, his grip tightening.

I swallow, feeling the ridge of each strong finger squeezing my throat in its grip. I suck in a shallow breath, my chest heaving.

"You don't scare me," I say, realizing my mistake as my voice quavers.

He chuckles before leaning down and pressing a rough kiss onto my waiting lips. He sucks in my bottom lip and then releases it with a pop. His hand tightens around my throat fractionally more as his gaze burns into mine. Dark spots flash behind my eyes and I am liquid in his arms. When he releases me, my body automatically screams for his return. For his heat. His grip. His kisses. For his cock... I squeeze my thighs together as the thoughts enters my head.

"One day soon," he promises with a dark glint in his eye, and then he leaves and I am trembling from head to toe in both fear and desire for him.

Chapter 8

Natalia

I find the wardrobe in my room is already filled with my clothes. At some point in the last 24 hours someone had all of my things brought here, and I'm grateful for that. That small piece of familiarity makes me feel more settled somehow. Despite being in a stranger's home with three dangerous men...two of whom have dragged several orgasms from me.

Dragged...really? I think with a scowl.

Amongst my own things are others that I don't recognize. Clothes that don't belong to me. Shoes that aren't mine. Yet I instinctively know that they are all for me. Everything is in my size and barring a few pieces which are far sexier than I would normally wear, I like them all.

I finger the garments that hang in the dressing room. Rack after rack of organized clothing, sorted into color and occasion. I pull out drawers and find underwear too, though all of this is brand new and I feel a blush rise to my cheeks as pull out each piece. Silk panties and lace bras. Corsets and suspenders. My cheeks flame hotter as I find a drawer with leather whips and nipple tassels. Clamps and body tape. I slam this drawer closed and press my back against it, as if fearing it could open all on its own.

I drag my hands down my face and swallow thickly, feeling confused and frightened but mostly excited by everything. I'm still unsure of who I belong to, and of what is expected of me, but as I stare around the room at the expensive clothing and silk underwear, at the drawers of gold jewelry and diamonds I know that this is a better prospect than what would have awaited me with Alfonso.

He would have taken what he wanted without wanting to please me. Where here, with these three men, it would seem at least, that my happiness...my pleasure is their aim.

I move around the room and pick out an outfit. Something new, as if releasing a new me. A new Natalia. I don't want to be the quiet obedient girl I once was. I want to be something more. Something fiercer for these men.

Downstairs I find Eva waiting in the kitchen for me and her face lights up when she sees me, her smile widening.

We make pancakes with what feels like a hundred

different toppings and then she takes me by the hand and begins to show me around her home. My home. Her mom sleeps the day away and as curious as I am to ask Eva about her mom, I don't. She seems so happy and carefree. Her small hand in mine as we walk around the lush grounds of the mansion.

"Daddy bought me a horse for my birthday," Eva says proudly as she leads me into the stables at the back of the mansion. She guides me to a soft gray mare with a white mane. It huffs and bobs its head as she comes closer. Its nose butting against the wooden gate that holds it in the stable.

"You can ride?" I say. "I'm impressed."

Eva shakes her head. "No. He got me lessons, but I was always too scared. She's called Buttercup and she's so pretty, but she's so big!"

Eva reaches up and strokes a hand down the horses' nose as it bows its head, its hoof kicking at the gate gently. I've always been fascinated by horses; their eyes seem to see the world with a clarity that seems impossible for me. But she's right...horses are huge and I've held a fear of falling from one for as long as I can remember.

"IT must be a daddy thing," I say and she turns to me with her inquisitive eyes. "Mine bought me a horse too, but I was a bit older. Can I tell you a secret?" I whisper and lean down putting my lips to her ear when she nods in excitement. "I can't ride either."

She laughs at this, finding the whole thing amusing.

I stroke my hand down Buttercup's nose with a smile, and when I glance down, I see that Eva is watching me.

"Would you like to ride her?" I ask and she bites down on the inside of her cheek and nods, her expression turning worried. "Maybe I could get my horse brought here and we could learn together."

Her worried expression turns to happiness and she nods again, releasing the inside of her cheek.

"Really?"

"Yes, really. My horse is called Enyo, and she is a beauty just like Buttercup."

Eva wraps her arms around my waist and hugs me and I feel warmth blossoming in my chest. When she pulls away, we share a silent moment with Buttercup before we turn to leave.

I'm surprised to see that it's past lunchtime now. The hours have passed quickly and I realize that I'm hungry. My stomach growls and we both laugh.

"Hungry?" I ask her and she nods.

We head back into the house and aim for the kitchen in search of food. However, as we pass through the main foyer, I hear raised voices coming from a room to the left. Eva looks up at me.

"That's daddy's office," she declares. "My brothers now

though..." her words trail off and I see the light go out of her eyes.

The voices have grown even louder, the odd word filtering out to us.

"...no!...For fucks sake, are you insane?...

"...don't say a damn thing!"

We both jump when the door is thrown open and Sisco storms out. He looks furious. His eyes ablaze with rage, his hair wild as he runs his hands through it, but his entire persona changes once he sees Eva and me and his mouth splits into a wild grin.

He comes to us quickly. "There's my two favorite girls." He wraps an arm round both of our waists and pulls us close. He buries his face in my neck and takes a deep breath, like he's sucking me into his lungs. "Hello, beautiful," he says, his voice already thick with lust.

Eva giggles and kicks out from under his grip. "Can't catch me!" she squeals excitedly and takes off running down the hallway.

Sisco lets her go, his lips now kissing along my throat. His other arm has come around me, tugging me tighter to him.

"You smell good enough to eat, Natalia," he moans against me, and I feel him hardening against my thigh as he pushes me backwards until my back hits the wall. Something wild and untamed unfurls in my stomach, heat

Claire C Riley

building in my core. He kisses along my throat, his hands cupping the sides of my face as his lips find their way there.

Sisco's eyes are like wild pools of raging water. Liquid danger that screams insanity whilst begging to be loved and I find myself completely at his mercy as he presses his hips into mine. His hard length grows harder still, and as his mouth finds mine, his tongue parting my waiting lips. He grinds himself against me and I sigh involuntarily.

My hands move to his hair, gripping it tightly as tingles electrify my body. From head to toe I am alive and silently begging for something I can't put a name too.

Our kisses have become wild and frantic, and Sisco reaches for the hem of my dress, readying to lift it and no doubt fuck me here on the stairs where anyone could see us when another voice sounds out behind him.

"Brother, I believe Eva is waiting for you to find her." It's Dominic. His stern voice splits the igniting passion between Sisco and I and Sisco pulls out of the kiss, his hands releasing my dress from their dexterous fingers.

Sisco presses his forehead against mine. "Another time, beautiful," he says breathlessly, and then he is gone. "I'm on my way!" he calls gleefully, almost childlike.

My cheeks are flaming red with desire and embarrassment as Dominic watches me with his attentive gaze. I reach up and straighten my hair and then my dress, before clearing my throat. I can't look him in the eye I realize, no matter how hard I try. And I wonder why that is.

He's seen me like this before...worse than this.

So why do I feel shame from his stern stare right now?

"Everything okay, little mouse?" he asks and I nod automatically, my voice suddenly lost.

Dominic takes a step towards me and I hold my breath. His suit jacket is undone, the top two buttons of his shirt undone. This is practically casual for him, and the thought makes me suddenly smirk.

His eyes widen at my smirk and the whole situation becomes suddenly comical and I laugh. The sound begins quietly at first until I'm laughing loudly. I clamp a hand over my mouth to hide my nervous laughter and try to get control of myself.

"Sorry," I mumble, not sure why I'm even laughing.

A smile tugs at the corner of his mouth and he looks like he's about to come to me when Joey steps out of the office.

"What the fuck are you doing out here, brother? We're in the middle of a meeting!" his eyes move from Dominic to me and then back again. "Never mind, we can finish up another time."

He turns to go back inside but Dominic pulls his gaze from mine and turns to his brother. "No, lets finish this."

"And Sisco?" Joey asks.

"He's playing with Eva. We'll fill him in later." He glances back to me. "Natalia," he says with a nod and then leaves.

The door to the office closes and I'm left alone in the quiet hallway, my thighs squeezing together and my chest still heaving. A smile plays on my lips still but I force it away and stand up before heading to find Eva and Sisco.

Chapter 9

Natalia

I wake to the feel of the bed dipping. I can't have been asleep for more than an hour, the fresh air of the day and the excitement of a new life taking its toll on me.

I open my eyes to find Sisco lying next to me. He's naked, his soft gray eyes watching me intently. He reaches over and trails a finger between my breasts, and there's no denying how hard my nipples are the moment he touches me. My skin is a blaze.

It's late, somewhere between midnight and morning, though the moon is still bright enough in the sky to illuminate his face for me.

"Is this okay?" he asks.

I don't know how to answer him. I don't even really

know what he's asking me.

Is it okay for him to be on my bed, touching me? My mind screams no, but my body screams yes. I'm fighting a war with myself and these men that I know I have no way to win. It's unfair, the advantage they have over me, but sometimes it's easier to let go than to fight every battle.

So I nod, yes, this is okay. For him to be here, with me, on my bed. Dominic said I'd be his soon, but soon isn't soon enough. And around these men I seem to have needs I've never had before.

"Do you have any idea how beautiful you are?" Sisco says, his finger still lazily trailing between my breasts. My nipples harden even further, and even in the darkness he must see what he does to me because a low rumble echoes from deep within his chest. He's like a barely restrained animal. "So beautiful," he murmurs.

He splays his huge hand out, cupping my breast in his palm and gently squeezing. I gasp as the soft material of my nightgown rubs against my sensitive nipples. He reaches up and pulls the thin strap down over my shoulder and down my arm, freeing my left breast. He plucks my hardened nipple between his fingers and I groan and arch my back, wanting more.

"You like that?" he asks, and after a moment's hesitation, I hum a yes.

I'm embarrassed to realize that I'm soaked for him

already, my most sensitive areas pulsing with the need for his touch. Desperate for his tongue. His fingers. Any part of him. But Sisco takes his time, teasing me every step of the way. He leans over me, flicking his tongue across my hardened nipple. His hand moves to free my other breast and I tangle both of my hands in his unruly hair, tugging on the longish locks. I need his mouth everywhere. His tongue, his teeth, his lips. I want him all over me. Devouring me. Savoring my desire.

He pushes the covers down my body and I automatically lift my knees up and open my legs for him. He chuckles against my flesh, his mouth peppering me with soft kisses.

"So eager," he rumbles, and I don't even care that he probably thinks I'm a slut right now. All I care about is the growing flame of desire inside of me.

Sisco moves down my body and I release his hair. He slides his tongue down my flesh, leaving a trail of damp in its wake. He moves lower until his mouth is at my pussy. He stills, and I'm poised and waiting, needing his tongue to touch me. To part my lips and spread me wide. Needing his fingers or his cock inside of me. I flinch as the vulgar word enters my head, but then I soften to it. Mold myself to it, adding more as I do.

His cock.

My pussy.

I want him to fuck me.

A thrill of desire courses through me, igniting my nerve ending as it goes. My body sparks and glows with hunger.

As the seconds pass, the moment becomes all the more urgent. Desire flares brighter in me and I buck my hips, hoping to find some friction.

"You want this, Natalia?" he asks, his words rumbling against my pussy and making me gasp.

"Oh god, yes!" I beg and plead.

His hands grip the sides of my panties, and he pulls them down my legs roughly and then drops his mouth to my body. Heat blazes against my skin as his mouth latches on to my clitoris and he sucks. My hands are back in his hair as he splits me wide with his tongue, lapping at me like I'm water from a fountain and he's dying of thirst.

I buck against his mouth. My hands pull on his hair as he flicks his tongue over and over me and I come, loudly, screaming into the air as pleasure hums through every part of me.

My nerves are on fire, every inch of me tingling and sensitive, desperate and eager. I hear the bedroom door opening and I open my eyes, finding Joey striding across the room towards the bed. If I were still the woman I was two days ago I would have been frightened by the fact that he was naked, his large, hard cock in his tattooed hand. But I wasn't that woman anymore. I'm so much more than that frightened little girl who had been promised to someone from the day she was born. Who had been told how to dress and how to speak and how to act. To protect her virtue. I was my own woman now. These men are giving me that gift. They are pleasuring me with their every breath. Their every touch. They are handing me strength on a silver platter and I take it in both hands.

I grasp my femininity and I carve it into what I want it to be. Who I want to be.

Sisco sits up, wiping his mouth with the back of his hand, his erection glistening in the moonlight as pre cum drips from the end of it.

Both men stare at me, eager, hungry for my touch, for my body, and it only takes me a second to decide my fate. To make my choice. Perhaps this was always the plan that fate had for me. Maybe this was always who I was meant to be. I'm happy with that thought.

I roll over and rise up to my knees, before leaning over to take Joeys' cock in my hand. My fingers wrap around it and I squeeze gently, strumming it before reaching over and sliding my mouth over it. Joey grunts as I take him deeply into the back of my throat, my fingers playing with the sensitive skin near his balls. I suck him hard, sheathing my teeth with my lips as he holds my hair and fucks into my mouth, gliding slowing into me over and over. He's slow at first, but his movements become more aggressive with each thrust.

I've never done this before, but I go with my instincts and do what comes natural to me, and it must be the right thing because unfathomably he seems to grow harder and bigger in my mouth. Joey grips my hair in his hands, fisting it in his grip as he thrusts over and over. My eyes water, but I open my throat, refusing to gag against the intrusion.

My body is still hypersensitive and tingling, my nipples like hard pebbles, as Sisco kneels behind me. I pause momentarily, Joey's cock still deep within my mouth as Sisco reaches around to squeeze my nipples, and then I'm groaning as desire hums through me.

Sisco rubs his hands over my back and over my ass, playfully slapping my backside, and then as Joey slides his cock all the way to the back of my throat, Sisco lines himself up with my entrance and slowly pushes himself inside of me. I moan, a feral sound that comes from deep inside. I'm an animal, my baser desires flaring to life.

I'm full to the brim with Sisco and Joey, taking each of them to the hilt as they take it in turns to rock into me, their movements slow at first, as if not wanting to rush toward their own orgasm but instead wanting to enjoy every second of it with me. Joey speeds up first, his hips bucking faster and faster as his hands grip my hair tighter. I look up at him through my lashes, seeing his heady, hungry gaze on me. He seems mesmerized by me. His lips parted, his hair hanging to one side as I taste the first of his cum at the back of my throat, and he calls out my name as I milk him for every drop.

When he's done, he slides himself out of my mouth and I drop to my elbows, raising my ass up higher, eager for my own release. Sisco begins fucking me harder and faster. His hand finds my ass as he squeezes and then slaps the cheeks. I grunt as the first flickers of an orgasm hit me before igniting like fireworks. Joey is running his hands through my hair and over my back as Sisco fucks me from behind, and when I think about it . . . really think about what is happening, and what has become of the pure, virginal princess that I once was, I come again with another loud scream, my pussy clenching around Sisco's cock. He hisses, bending his body over mine, his arms wrapping around me. He kisses along my back, licking and nipping my flesh as his hips rock back and forth and then he kneels back up and grinding into me as he fills me to the hilt and comes with a loud roar.

I'm a whimpering, well-fucked wreck when he gently slides himself out of my sensitive body and I collapse onto my front. I've lost all ability to talk as Joey climbs onto the bed with me, pulling me to his chest. I lay my head there, my breath still coming in heaving pants, my body still shuddering with the aftershocks of pleasure.

Several moments pass and then Sisco climbs into bed too. I don't have the energy to ask him what's happening.

He pulls the covers up to keep us all warm, and between these two men's arms I fall into the deepest, most satisfied sleep of my life.

Chapter 10

Dominic

"**Y**ou need to go and see your father," I say sternly, too sternly. The words feel like a bitter betrayal as they leave my mouth.

Natalia's hair is still mussed around her face, her eyes still filled with tiredness. I see the confusion cross her face. The worry as she wonders if she's done something wrong. Perhaps thinking of the previous night she spent with my brothers. I love that look on her face; both shame and hunger for more, and I would love nothing more than to fuck it off her face, but this isn't the time for that and I hate the news I have to give her.

"Natalia, your father had another heart attack. He's back in the hospital so we should leave immediately so that you can be with him."

"My father?" she's still tired from sleep but the realization slowly dawns on her and she gasps.

"Get dressed. I'll meet you by the car," I say and she leaves quickly.

I head out into the hallway, seeing the shadow of my mother heading towards the kitchen.

"Everything okay?" I call to her and she stops and turns to look at me.

She looks broken, like always, but there's more clarity in her eyes today. She comes to me, pressing a strong hand to the side of my face.

"My beautiful boy," she coos, and I reach up and take her hand in mine, before bringing it to my lips. I kiss the back of her hand and she smiles. Her eyes pierce me, her smile soft. "So handsome." She leans over and presses a kiss to my cheek and then turns and leaves and I stare after her longingly.

Turning on my heel, I head to the limousine, and wait for Natalia there. Satisfied when she doesn't keep me waiting long. A hungry smile flits to my face as she walks towards me, unable to hide the slight limp she has. Yes, Sisco and Joey definitely helped her settle into her new home last night.

I've already told Angelo, my driver and most trusted guard, where we will be going and he sets off as soon as the doors are closed.

It's mid-afternoon, and I'd had one of my guards wake her. The last week had apparently taken its toll on my little mouse.

She hasn't spoken yet, and I give her time to gather her thoughts as we ride in silence, her gaze outside while I can barely take my eyes off of her. Joey and Sisco are out dealing with the Russians again. Apparently, they weren't quite done with our dealings yet and we have one more duty we have to take care of before our businesses can part ways. I hate it, but it's necessary. I need to protect my family at all costs, and the Russians can't be trusted.

Right now, I'm holding on to too many secrets for my liking, but like the Russians, they're necessary to keep. At least for the moment.

I watch her carefully, wondering what's going on in that pretty head of hers. She's hard to read when she's like this; closed off and lost in her own thoughts. I want nothing more than to tell her that it will be okay. That her father will pull through and all will be well in her world once again. But I can't make that promise to her. I can't take away her pain or her worry. The realization that I can't control this situation for her, that I can't protect her from the inevitable, is a bitter pill to swallow.

My cell rings when we're two minutes from the hospital, and I answer it, listening carefully to the voice on the other end. When I hang up, I see that she's watching me expectantly, beautiful wide eyes staring at me because she already knows what's coming.

"He's gone, isn't he?" she says, her voice flat.

I could lie to her, but to what end. She'd find out in a matter of moments anyway.

I put my cell phone away and nod. "Yes, I'm afraid so, Natalia."

She goes back to staring out the window until we pull up outside the hospital and then I help her out. Her steps are unsteady and I wrap an arm around her waist as we walk inside.

"Do you want to sit down for a moment?" I ask, slowing us to a stop. "You don't have to go up if you don't want to. I can take you home. Whatever you want."

She shakes her head. "I need to see him."

"Very well." I nod.

I walk with her until we reach the floor her father is on and then I stop. Her father's bodyguards are outside of his room so she'll be well looked after. She turns to look at me as I pull to a stop.

"You're not coming with me?" she asks uncertainly.

I shake my head. "I'll give you some space to be with him," I say. "To say your goodbyes."

"What if I don't come back to you? What will you do then?" she asks.

I reach out, placing my fingers on the bottom of her chin and tilt her face up to look me in the eye. "You're not my prisoner, Natalia."

"Am I not?" she asks, her tone almost conflicted.

There's fire in her eyes and I lean down and press my lips to hers. She doesn't pull away and I don't give anything further than a brief touch of contact before pulling away.

"You have never been my prisoner, though I won't deny the thought of you being tied up and at my mercy is somewhat thrilling." I release her chin, sliding my hands into my suit pockets. "I'll be downstairs when you're ready."

Her eyes fill with unshed tears and she nods before walking away, her footsteps still unsteady.

I feel like a piece of shit leaving her to deal with this on her own, but I know she's strong enough to. And I know she needs to come to terms with his loss by herself. Outside the room are a couple of Frank's security guys. She hugs them when she reaches them and the sight of their hands on her make me bristle. She goes inside Franks room and I hear the first soft sob leave her throat before the door is closed behind her. Turning, I head back the way we just came, intending on waiting in the limousine for her. Back downstairs I see Angelo stood by the entrance waiting for us and I head in his direction.

He notes that Natalia isn't with me and raises an eyebrow in question.

"She needs time to come to terms with her loss," I say by way of explanation. By his expression I guess that he also thought Natalia was my prisoner and is surprised that I let her out of my sight. "Does she drink coffee?" I ask.

He pulls out his cell and phones the house to ask the housekeeper. Moments later he slides his cell back into his jacket.

"Coffee, one sugar, plenty of milk," he replies. "There's a Starbucks a block from here. Should I go and get it for her?"

I shake my head. "No, I'll go. You stand guard, I don't trust the Rosso's not to show their faces."

He raises an eyebrow at that too, but I ignore him and head back out into the bright day. The Starbucks is as Angelo said, only a short block away, and the walk does me good. It clears my head. I make a brief call to Sisco to check on the Russian deal, happy enough when he tells me that everything is going as planned.

"Where are you?" he asks suddenly.

I've just slipped out of Starbucks, coffee in hand, as I walk back to the hospital. "I'm going back for her now," I state.

"Are you walking, brother? Why are you walking?" he sounds bemused.

"The hospital has many ears," I reply sharply.

Sisco chuckles. "Did you just go to a Starbucks?" he

says with another chuckle and I give a heavy sigh.

"What the fuck have I told you about tracking my phone, brother?" I snap, but he's not listening anymore. He's called Joey over and is informing him of the situation. Apparently, they think I'm pussy-whipped. It would be insulting if I wasn't inclined to agree with them. Not that I would ever admit to that. Joey, from the bark of laughter that echoes through the phone, also thinks it's highly amusing that I've just walked to Starbucks instead of having Angelo go for me.

I hang up without further reply.

I momentarily doubt my decision to fetch Natalia coffee, wondering what the fuck I'm doing. But that's what normal people do in these situations, right? Get coffee, or tea, and then sit and mourn the loss of their loved ones. That's what should happen. Only it's never been like that for me. It's always been blood and death following more blood and death. It's never-ending, the flow of it through our family.

I need it to end.

I need it to be over with.

Once and for all.

I'm holding her coffee tight in my grip as I enter the hospital once again, giving Angelo a quick nod. I want to make her feel better, but I don't know how I can. She's just lost her father, the only man she's ever loved. The man that raised her and gave her the world. There can be no way to fix that for her, but I'll start with roses. I call a florist on my way back up to Frank's floor and arrange for twelve dozen roses to be delivered to the house, and then I phone the house and tell the maids to arrange the flowers in her room.

Angelo is following behind me and I'm deeply aware that he can hear every word I say, but he makes no comment.

The roses will be a nice surprise for her, but I know it isn't enough, and I'm thinking of what else I can do as I stop at the end of the hallway and see all of Frank's security is missing. I immediately place the coffee down by my feet and pull out my gun before slowly making my way down the hallway toward his room. Angelo is right behind me, his own gun in hand.

When I get to the room, I see a deathly still Frank in his bed but there's no one else around. I briefly worry that she will have left. I did just tell her that she wasn't my prisoner after all. I'd never assumed that she would take that as her right to leave me though.

Angelo taps me on the shoulder and points towards the stairs and I nod. The doorway to the stairs is on one side of the hallway and there is an office on the other. Angelo heads into the office, his gun at eye level. I push open the stairway door and immediately hear voices, and I quietly close the door behind me, taking the steps down as silently as I can.

"Don't get too comfy, cara mia, you'll be back where you

belong soon enough," Alfonso snarls.

I look down and see he has my Natalia against the wall, his face an inch from hers. She's whimpering as he presses himself against her, and I see red with rage.

"Make sure you save yourself for me. I've waited a long time for this." He presses his hand between her legs and I watch as she winces—whether it be from his mere touch or because of Sisco's cock last night I'm not sure, and I don't care. Natalia is mine, ours, and I'll kill any man that lays a finger on her.

"You've given it to them already!" he snarls in her face, his anger making him deaf to my steps as I storm toward him, my gun raised. "Never mind, instead of having a princess for a wife, now I'll have a whore to keep my bed warm." Alfonso leans in and presses a brutal, unforgiving kiss to her mouth, and she cries out in pain just as I reach them.

I slam the barrel of my gun into the back of his head and he releases her and turns on me. His hand goes for the gun at his waist, but mine is already out and from the look on my face he knows he's seconds away from dying. Natalia is crying, tears pouring freely down her cheeks.

"Come," I say, and gesture for her to move away from him.

She comes to my side automatically, pressing herself against my back.

"I should kill you where you stand," I growl at him.

He's glaring at me, his hand still itching to go for his gun. I almost want him to. It would certainly make things easier. But this isn't the time or the place for death. Natalia is fragile, she's just seen her dead father, and this hospital doesn't need more dead bodies than it already has.

"Go on then," he taunts, his neck corded with barely contained rage. "If you think you're man enough to do it."

"I think we both know now that I'm man enough," I say with a sneer.

His face, if possible, turns even redder with rage as he glances at Natalia. He doesn't need to know that I've barely touched the girl yet. That I allowed my brothers to defile her, yet I've never even seen her naked. He makes the assumption all on his own and I allow his thoughts to run wild.

"Such a dirty whore," he seethes.

I click off the safety and his gaze comes back to me. "You don't look at her, Alfonso. You don't even think about her."

"Or what?" he yells.

Angelo has come and joined me, and I see from my peripheral vision that he has his gun aimed at Alfonso too.

"Your time is coming, mark my words," I say between ragged, angry breaths. "But not today...not like this."

Alfonso takes one last look at Natalia, and there's no denying the longing he still has for her. The jealousy he feels that I have her. "I'll be back to collect what's mine," he says to me, and then turns and leaves.

I want nothing more than to shoot him in the back of the head as he walks away and damn the consequences, but I hold my temper. His time is soon, and I'll take great joy in his death.

When he's gone, I turn back to Natalia, seeing the blood on her lips from where he kissed her so hard that her lip has split. I put my gun away and reach down, scooping her up in my arms easily and then I march back up the stairs with Angelo close behind. She leans her head against my chest, sobbing quietly against me.

"Where are your fathers' men?" I ask as we pass Franks room.

"I don't know," she whispers between sobs.

I carry her all the way back to the limousine, even holding her on my lap once we're back inside it. It's only then that she mercifully stops crying. I don't even know what's making her cry anymore—her father's death or what that bastard just did to her. All I know is that I'd do anything to make her stop. Hearing her in so much pain is fucking killing me.

I stroke her back gently all the way back to the house, kissing the top of her head gently. Once inside I carry her up to her room and place her on the bed. I unbutton my jacket and go to her bathroom and run her a bath before returning for her. She's staring around her in amazement, gazing at the roses on every surface. I swallow apprehensively. I didn't expect to be here to see her reaction, but now that I am, I pray that she'll like it.

She looks up at me. "You did this?" she asks, and I nod.

I reach down and pull her up to standing, leading her to the bathroom. She looks in at the warmth bath filled with sweet-scented bubbles.

"I ran you a bath. I thought it might help relax you."

"Thank you," she says, her voice a hoarse whisper.

I turn to leave but she reaches out and grips my wrist in her tiny hands. I look back at her sharply, my jaw ticking.

"Stay," she says, her eyes pleading.

We stare at one another for a long moment before I dare speak. "What are you asking me, Natalia? Be very clear about this."

Her cheeks are flushed as she releases my hand. She reaches to her side and slowly unzips her dress. As the material hits the floor, she steps out of it and pushes it away with her foot. Her hands move to her underwear, unclipping her bra and letting it fall at her feet before she reaches down and slides her panties down her silky thighs. I suck in a breath, my cock already pulsing.

She stands in front of me naked, her face still flushed from crying, and her chin held high. But I don't look at her body—not yet. Instead, I hold her gaze, my expression impassive.

"What are you asking me, Natalia? Tell me what you

want," I say, refusing, even now in her misery to back down from our unspoken torment. I reach out and curl a length of hair around one of my fingers and she shivers. "I won't touch you without you asking me to."

Her tongue darts out to wet her lips, and my cock hardens. "Stay with me." She glances toward the bath. "Be with me."

I cup the side of her face in my hand, my fingers tangling in her hair as I drag her closer to me and our gazes collide. It's a split second before I press my mouth to hers, rougher than I meant for it to be because she whimpers, the split lip from Alfonso coming open and her blood mixing in our mouths.

When I pull my lips away, she's panting, and I release her and undress, not giving a damn that my suit gets dropped to the floor. She takes my hand and leads me to the bath before climbing in and turning to me. The bathroom is huge, the bath more like a small pool and she sinks into the water, bubbles surrounding her. Her eyes finally fall to my heavy cock and she gasps, her pupils dilating at the sight of it.

She's stunning in that moment—nipples hard, eyes wide and begging, chest heaving. I step into the bath and sit down before pulling her to me, dragging her down until she's positioned over my heavy, throbbing cock.

"Tell me again," I order her, holding her gaze. "Tell me

you want it. That you want me."

She reaches between us and grasps my cock in her hand, holding it tightly in her palm. "I want you, Dominic. I want you inside of me, please," she implores. "Make the pain go away, even if it's just for a moment."

Chapter 11

Dominic

I wrap my hands around her throat and squeeze, her mouth opens and she sucks in a frightened breath. The sight makes my cock harder in her grip and she groans even as she struggles for breath, her hands moving up and down my length.

The feeling is exquisite, but it's not what I want.

"Enough," I snap and she lets go, placing her hands on my chest in total obedience. I release one hand from her throat and she gasps and sucks in a ragged breath. Reaching down between us, I press three thick fingers at her entrance. Her gaze is on mine and it widens as I push my fingers inside her, hooking them to reach the spot I know is there, just out of reach.

Natalia groans again, and I lean up and suck a hard nipple into my mouth as I flick my fingers back and forth. With each groan she elicits my excitement grows until I feel the insanity of need and desire pulsing through me.

I can't wait another second.

I slide my fingers out and sit back, before gripping her hips and slamming her down on my hard length in one abrupt move. My hand is still at her throat and as she opens her mouth wide, a scream beginning to escape I squeeze my fingers tightly, snapping the sound off.

My cock is buried deep inside her, and I feel her pulsing need squeezing my cock. She swallows and then her hips begin to move slowly, rocking me in her warmth. I raise an eyebrow but say nothing, allowing her to fuck me.

"Oh...Dominic..." she hums my name and the sound of it spilling from her lips makes something animalistic inside of me flair to life.

I grip her hips in my large palms and lift her up before pulling her back down on me. I stretch her tight pussy wide as I fill her completely, plunging myself into her warm depths over and over. She whimpers, gasping at the ferocity of the intrusion and the sound spurs me on. I want nothing more than to fuck her hard and fast, making her cum on me with an ear-splitting scream.

I sit up, sucking her breast into my mouth again, and nibble on the hard pebble. I cup them in my large hands, kneading them, and pull on her nipples until she clenches around me with another soft whimper.

Her hands roam down my hard chest, moving over every defined muscle as I continue to palm her breasts and fuck up into her, the bathwater cascading to the floor. Her pussy squeezes me greedily. I hiss and her gaze flies to mine. It encourages her and her hips begin to rock back and forth, gently at first, until she starts to build momentum.

She's never done this before, but there's something even more seductive about that. Something beautiful about her innocence as she rocks on me, eager to please, desperate to learn. I scoop up the warm water and trail it down her chest as she continues to build momentum. She's beautiful. An angel as the water laps around us while she rides me.

Reaching up I clasp her face in my hands before pinning her hair back from her face and pull her mouth to mine. We collide together in tongues and teeth, greedy and desperate.

Her hips buck with a hard thrust, her nails slicing down my chest. The more I groan or hiss, the harder she fucks me, until water is splashing all around us and she's fucking me hard and fast, searching for her own release. She lifts herself up and then slams herself down onto me as her pussy squeezes me tighter and she calls out some garbled nonsense.

I feel her throbbing around me, pulsing with her orgasm as we continue to kiss. Tongues colliding hungrily.

When her movements slow to almost nothing I grab her by the hips and lift her off of me, carrying her to the bedroom on heavy, wet feet. I throw her onto the bed and she squeals, excitement and thrill flushing her cheeks. She smiles up at me as I climb onto the bed and she scrambles up higher, but I chase her until I catch her. Grasping her by the ankles and pull her to me, spreading her legs wide as I settle myself between them. My hard length is heavy against her entrance and she writhes under me playfully until I buck my hips abruptly and slam myself in to the hilt, filling her up in one swift move.

"Oh god!" she calls out as I lift her legs, raising them to my shoulders as I find greater depths than before and begin to brutally pound into her. I wrap one arm around her legs, keeping them close to my chest, the other reaches between us and presses against her clit. She closes her eyes as I fuck her hard and fast, the bed pounding against the wall loudly. My balls are desperate to be emptied, it's been months since I came, but I want this moment to last so I force myself to slow down, instead, rocking into her slowly.

I hear the door open and close behind me and the sound of my brothers undressing, and then they both climb onto the bed with us. Her eyes fly open, taking in the sight of all three of us, and I see the panic in her eyes at first before it settles slowly into ease again. Joey presses his mouth to hers and she kisses him back, her hand in his hair. Sisco takes her breast in his mouth, biting gently on her nipple until she moans into Joey's mouth. I fuck into her, her body used to my size now, but still tight enough that she's squeezing me tightly. She's so wet she's soaking the sheets beneath us and I roll my hips as I slide in and out of her with ease.

Joey lies down on his back, his hands behind his head, and I slide out of her. She watches me warily, unsure what I'm asking of her, so I guide her up and onto his lap. He aims himself at her entrance and pushes himself in, and she places her hands on his chest and starts to move on him, gathering momentum with every buck of her hips. I gather the moisture from my cock and spread her ass cheeks before rubbing the moisture around her asshole. She stops moving and turns to look at me with panic in her eyes.

"Trust me, Natalia," I soothe gently as I press a finger against her asshole and slowly push it inside her.

She groans and Joey lifts his hips, pushing himself inside of her again. She looks back down at him as I slide my finger in and out, widening her asshole for me as he fucks her pussy.

When I think she's ready, and I can take no more waiting, I press my hardened cock against her ass, and with a low growl I push myself inside her.

Chapter 12

Natalia

I've never felt anything like it as Dominic pushes his large cock slowly into my ass. My body clings to him too tightly and he winces. Pain vibrates through me mixed with the pleasure of Joey in my pussy. I whimper, eager, frightened, desperate for more. For less. For everything.

Dominic kisses my shoulder, pushing himself further inside me. "Relax, Natalia, relax," he urges, his voice a husky whisper against my flesh.

Sisco leans over to kiss me, his hand going to my clitoris and pressing on it. It feels good, so good that I forget for a moment that Dominic has his cock in my ass and Joey has his cock in my pussy.

Sisco rubs and flicks my clitoris and my body slowly

settles with the two men. Joey starts to move again, his hips rising up to fuck me, and then Dominic starts to move slowly, pushing himself all the way into me and then pulling all the way out. I've never felt so full in all my life.

My body is pulsing.

It's on fire.

It's electrified with desire as the two men fuck me. My head hangs low to my chest, and all I can do is sit there and be fucked in every hole.

It's too good.

It's too much.

With every stroke I don't think I can take any more. It's too intense and I can't do anything but sit there in a daze as they take what they need from me and also give me everything and more in return.

I don't even know that I'm crying until Sisco kisses the salty tears from my cheeks. His hand is still at my clitoris, his other hand tugging roughly on his thick cock. With trembling hands, I reach over and take over from him. He kneels up on the bed, close enough for me to lean over and take him into my mouth, but in doing so it gives both Dominic and Joey greater depth inside of me and all four of us groan in unison.

Sisco fucks my mouth, his cock reaching well into my throat with every thrust. His hands are in my long hair, knotting it around his fists so he can see my face as he slides in and out of my mouth. Dominic fucks into my ass, his huge body leaning over my small one as he rocks in and out quicker and quicker, deeper and deeper. Kissing my shoulder and neck, biting on my earlobe and whispering reassurances into my ears. And Joey ruts his hips up to meet mine as he pounds into my pussy over and over, his hands on my hips. He hisses through his teeth, his grip tightening on me as I begin to speed up.

I'm so close I can see the crest of my orgasm in the distance and I'm eager to get there. To feel the tidal wave of delirium wash over me like a heavy blanket.

Every part of me is filled to the brim. I'm overflowing with these men. With their pleasure. Their desire. I'm ignited with the power of it and the need of it all. And I'm greedy for more.

The feeling begins in my toes, traveling up my legs until it reaches my pussy and ass, and then my nipples go even harder as the euphoria takes over and the tidal wave hits me. I come with a cry that is almost a sob, but it won't stop. The orgasm keeps on coming over and over, getting harder and harder as all three men fuck into me. As one orgasm hits and starts to slide away, another one grows in its place. The cycle continues as they slide in and out of my body, hot and hard. Until I can't take it anymore and I feel like I'm going crazy. It's too much and I need it to stop almost as much as I want more. I pull on Sisco's cock, sucking him hard, desperate for nothing and everything all at once. His grip tightens on my hair until it's painful. Until he's coming down my throat in long hot splashes, and then I release him with a loud pop from my mouth as I grunt and flick my hips, slamming both Dominic and Joey's cocks into my center roughly.

They both call out and it's all I need to encourage me. I do it again and again and again, the insanity of desire and pleasure taking over until I'm fucking both of them, my body a temple and my mind free of its shackles for the first time ever.

I fuck them both until they both call out loudly, expanding and stretching me wider as they come in long, hot spurts, dousing my insides. Dominic is breathless and shuddering as he throbs inside my ass. He slowly slides out and then rolls away, breathless. He lies on the bed, his damp chest heaving as he looks at me. An expression I can't describe on his handsome face.

Joey is still inside of me. He's still hard and I can feel his cum sliding out between our bodies. I'm trembling, my body spent and exhausted. Unnerved by myself as much as I am about these men.

I think that we're done. My body is trembling, its reserves depleted and I'm about to climb off Joey but Sisco kneels behind me and before I can say anything he slams himself in deep in my ass.

I scream in both pleasure and pain at the sudden intrusion.

I look over my shoulder at him as Joey reaches up, his fingers finding my mouth. He runs his thumb along my bottom lip as I stare at Sisco, my mouth open in a gasp, my eyes watering.

I can't take any more.

I can't not take any more.

I want all of it, everything that these men have to give me.

I never want it to stop.

"Please," I whisper, sucking Joey's thumb into my mouth.

Sisco places his hands on my shoulders and I lean my head to the side, resting my cheek against his tattooed hands.

Sisco fucks me for what seems like forever. Until time and space don't exist anymore and my body is a temple of pleasure. Joey is still soft inside of me, but he grows harder with each thrust of Sisco, until he begins to move and fuck me to.

Cocks slide in and out of my body over and over, until each man becomes a blur. It's Joey that's fucking me, and then it's Dominic again. He's wider and he stretches me almost painfully. And the whole time, Sisco is behind me, hands wrapped around me, nipping at my flesh while he fucks my ass.

I come again, several times, we all do. And then I pass out in a tangle of beautiful limbs that wrap me in their embrace. I sleep for what feels like a hundred years, my body sore and well spent, my mind soothed and calm for the first time in years.

I've never felt so desired and happy, and I realize that I wouldn't want to be anywhere else but here, in their arms.

Chapter 13

Dominic

I sip on my bourbon, my gaze on the fire burning inside the fireplace in my father's study. I'm bare-chested, with only a pair of dress pants on and feeling completely comfortable in my own home for the first time in years. It's late and everyone is sleeping but me. I like this time to myself though. It's my time to gather my thoughts and reconcile my actions for the day. Normally I'm putting to rest the dark things I've done that day—dark things that have usually ended in blood and death—but not tonight.

Tonight, I'm thinking of Natalia.

Not just her body, but her, Natalia, and everything that makes her. I don't like secrets. Secrets are the sins of the Devil, and they bring nothing but misery. But I have a secret so big that it could blow up our very happiness, and it's making me sick. One secret leads to another secret and another, until it's just a spindle of lies and deceit.

I need to tell her the truth, I realize with dark dread.

Natalia has become something special to us all, including Eva and our mom. She's one of us now, and I can't keep these secrets from her for much longer—not if we want to keep her. If she finds out on her own, she'll never forgive me.

The sound of footsteps outside the door has me looking up, and I watch as the handle turns and Sisco walks in. He's never been much of a sleeper, but I would have thought that after tonight he would have slept like the dead.

"Brother," he grunts, strutting across the room to get himself a drink.

He's barefoot too and wearing only a T-shirt and boxer briefs. Once he has a drink, he sits opposite me and drags a hand down his sleepy face, trying to wake himself up.

"What time is it?" he asks.

I check my Rolex. "One thirty," I reply, and take another sip.

We sit in comfortable silence for a while, each of us lost in our own thoughts, and it's not long before Joey comes down to meet us too.

"Oh for fuck's sakes, brothers, can't I get a moment's peace to myself?" I say with only a touch of annoyance.

For as far back as I can remember, my brothers and I have shared everything. We should have been triplets; our bond is that strong. We've been each other's shadows through the years; where one of us goes, the others usually follow shortly after. But I never thought we'd find a woman to mutually satisfy all three of us. But Natalia, my sweet Natalia, has turned out to be completely perfect in every way.

"Tell me we're keeping her, brother," Joey says ignoring my outburst. He pours himself a shot of vodka and throws it to the back of his throat before pouring a second one right after. "Dominic?"

He sounds desperate and he looks it when he turns to me. He won't give her up without a fight if that were going to be the case. But it's not.

My gaze moves to Sisco in question, and he nods in agreement with Joey. "I'm not letting her go either. She's one of us now. Maybe she always has been."

"And if she doesn't want to stay?" I ask. "What then?"

Sisco laughs crudely. "Were you upstairs with us earlier? Did it seem like she wanted to get away from us?"

I sigh. "It's all well and good in the dark of night, but in the stark reality of daylight, people have a way of changing their minds."

"Then we'll lock her in the fucking basement until she changes her mind!" Sisco snaps, his eyes ablaze with madness and excitement at the prospect. "She's ours, forever. I can't let her go, not now, brother!"

"Not after that," Joey agrees with a jerk of his head upstairs. He's more serious and subdued, but he'll stand by Sisco's side in this.

I stand up and walk to my desk, my bare feet padding on the wooden floors. "What you're talking about is kidnapping an innocent woman and forcing her to fuck us for the rest of her life. I've done many terrible things in my life, brothers, but that won't be one of them."

Sisco comes over and pats me on the shoulder, a smirk on his face. "No, what we're talking about is convincing her that she should stay with us."

"That she belongs with us," Joey adds on, his expression serious.

"She does belong with us, Dom. You know it as well as we do. It's like she was made just for us," Sisco says matter-of-factly.

I sigh. Heavy is the head that wears the crown I suppose.

"She is everything we could have ever hoped for, I'll give you that. But it has to be her choice. She has to want to stay with us. All three of us. Her whole life up until this point has been orchestrated for her. This can't be like that." I wrestle with the words in my head, unsure how to get them out. It's Joey who says them with clarity for me.

"You want better for her," he states.

"More for her," Sisco adds. "Then let us give it to her. We can give her anything and everything, Dom, you know this."

"It's not about trinkets, brother. It's more than that and you know it. She's fucking special." The words burst from me, sounding almost angry. "She needs to know the truth. Only then can she make her decision."

Sisco takes step towards me, his expression turning angry. "Don't you fucking dare!"

"She'll leave, Dominic. You know she will. Why would you risk her for that? To ease your fucking conscience? Don't act like you're whiter than white. Like you don't have blood on your hands." Joey has come closer, his anger growing with each passing word. "You may want to make us legit. To stop the bloodshed and war, but death will always surround you. You can't hide who you are, brother."

"Enough!" I yell, standing up straighter and taking a step towards him. "Who the fuck do you think you're talking to? I know I have blood on my hands, blood I don't even try to clean off because it's who I am. I own that. I accept that. I know who I am. But this...keeping her without her knowing all the facts, that's not fucking happening. If she wants to go, she can go. I won't let either of you keep her here without her consent."

Sisco snorts out a laugh and takes a step towards the door. "I'll prep the basement for her," he throws over his shoulder, "she's not going fucking anywhere. She's mine... ours!"

I slam my glass on the table. "God damn it, brothers. Listen to yourselves! You can't force her to love you."

Joey sneers at me. "I can fuck her until she loves me. Until she wants to stay. I'll pleasure her body in ways she's never dreamed possible, until her every waking breath is for me. Until she doesn't want to leave because all she can think about is me!"

"I want to stay," Natalia says quietly from the doorway.

We all turn to look at her, my breath stolen from my lungs when I see her standing there. She's wearing my dress shirt, her hair wild and untamed with an air of just-fuckedness about it. Her cheeks are still flushed, her lips swollen. A low growl begins in my chest automatically and her cheeks flush redder. Sisco and Joey have stopped in their tracks, both of them eyeing her like lions waiting to pounce.

"I've never felt like that before," she says, her voice hesitant. "So wanted, so in control of... everything."

She comes closer to us, and as she draws near, Joey hands her his glass of vodka. She takes it with a shy smile and my dick twitches at the sight.

"My whole life I've been told what to do, where to go, who to talk to, how to talk, but that upstairs . . . that was . . ."

Joey touches the bottom of her glass and she nods and

takes a sip while she gathers her thoughts.

"I chose that," she says firmly. "I wanted that . . . you . . . all of you."

"You should sleep on it," I say, and Sisco turns to me with a scowl.

"Will you shut the fuck up, brother!"

"It's a big decision." I lean back against the desk, my hands gripping the edges of it. "Once you decide, there's no going back from it." In truth, I don't think I could let her go now either. She's deep within the viper's nest and the exits are blocked.

"I don't need to sleep on it." She throws the rest of the vodka to the back of her throat and swallows. "I know what I want."

I smirk. "Be sure, because now they've had a taste of you my brothers won't let you go without a fight."

"And you?" she says coming closer. "Will you let me go without a fight, Dominic?" she undoes the highest button on my shirt, showing more skin. My mouth quirks, desire flooding me. What was it with this woman that made me throw all sense and reasoning out of the window?

"Careful, little mouse," I warn her, my cock hardening as she undoes another button.

"Why do I always have to convince you to touch me?"

I chuckle. "Natalia, there is no convincing necessary. Right now, I'm imagining you bent over my desk with your ass in the air. Trust me when I say I want you. I just want you to be sure that you know what you're letting yourself in for. There are things we need to tell you. Things that could change your mind."

"Then don't tell me," she says firmly. "I don't want to know if it's going to ruin this...us. I'm happy, for the first time in my life, I'm truly happy. Don't ruin that for me, Dominic." She places her hands at the bottom of the shirt that she's wearing, lifting it to show that she's not wearing any panties. I hear Sisco's sharp intake of breath.

"I know what I want and that's you—all of you," she says with resolution. "No amount of sleep is going to change my mind." She looks between all three of us, her gaze finally fixing on me.

"Then it's settled," Sisco says before I can say anything else. His grin grows wide and wolfish, all sleepiness gone from his eyes.

Joey looks between us as if deciding what is right and wrong and then deciding if he gives a fuck.

I don't feel good about the decision, though I know I should. We have everything now. The money, the empire, the power, and the woman. We have everything men could ever want and more.

"Dominic—," she begins, her hand darting between her legs, but then lights suddenly pierce the dimness of the room and I frown and turn to the window. The lights grow brighter as headlights come closer, and I know then that it's too late to stop this from happening.

"Down! Now!" I roar, grabbing Natalia and dragging her to the ground. Joey is closest to Sisco and he pulls our brother down with him.

Seconds later, the windows explode inward as guns go off outside. Natalia screams, but all I can do is drape my body over hers to protect her from the falling glass and debris. Sisco and Joey are crawling over to the safe to get our guns as the roar of gunfire continues all around us.

Glass rains down on us all, windows imploding from the bullets, peppering the walls and artwork of our father's office. It seems never ending. A constant din roar of bullets exploding, tearing apart our home in search for us.

Natalia is shaking and crying and the glass is sprinkling against our bare flesh. Small shards stick in me creating streaks of blood, but I feel nothing but rage.

"Dom!" Sisco calls, and I look up, watching as he slides a gun across the floor to me. I reach an arm out, grabbing it firmly in my grip.

Natalia looks over her shoulder into my face, her wide eyes imploring me to make it all stop, and my anger increases until I can barely contain it. I feel like an inferno ready to explode. I'm going to fucking kill every bastard that thought they could come to my home and try to kill me and the people that I love.

Every single one of them is going to die.

"Give me another," I yell, and Joey slides over another gun to me.

The gunfire stops and I hear doors opening and closing outside as the people—whoever the fuck they are—climb out of their cars, coming inside to rain more gunfire down on us. I grip Natalia's hand and push the gun into her palm, flicking off the safety.

"I can't," she sobs, and my features harden.

"You can," I tell her with steel in my voice so she knows that there's no room for argument. "And you will. Aim, squeeze . . ."

"And kill," Sisco says firmly from the other side of the room.

She glances over at Joey, who holds her gaze steady and raw, and then she bites down on her bottom lip and nods. I hold my hand up, warning everyone to wait as the front door is repeatedly kicked as they attempt to get inside. My gaze strays to Sisco, who's like a coiled spring, ready to jump up and kill everything and everyone in his path. He wears a grin that splits his face, his eyes full of wild mania. Joey has his back to the safe, the gun against his chest as he mouths a prayer and kisses the cross that hangs around his neck.

As footsteps thunder down the hallway in search of us, I nod to my brothers, my family, my life, and I stand up.

Each of them follows, and we aim our guns at the door to the office. Mere seconds go by before the handle turns and the door opens wide, and then all four of us let fire with a hellish noise, releasing our ammo into every man that tries to get inside.

They don't stand a chance.

Blood sprays across the walls and floor, cries of pain and groans of anguish sound out. Wood splinters around us all and glass smashes. The house is torn apart in the war but none of us stop until every man that tried to enter is dead on the ground or running in the opposite direction.

Sisco takes off after them, giving a whoop of excitement. "Little pigs, little pigs...here I come!" he taunts.

Natalia's face is hard with determination, but once the last body drops she gasps, releasing the air in her lungs and holding the now empty gun out to me with shaking hands. We stand silently, all of us half-naked, covered in blood splatter and staring in shock at the bodies piled in and around the doorway.

I hear gunshots outside and then a car screech away and fury builds in me that anyone made it out of this alive. The thought is infuriating. Several more gunshots echo through the night loudly. One outside and seconds later, two more in the hallway just outside this room. Then Sisco comes back in with his grin still in place. He looks untamed and exhilarated.

"Three got in a car and got away, but if I chase them now, I should catch up to them," he says breathlessly.

A man in the mound moves, and Sisco's grin widens. He grabs a knife from the open safe before straddling the man and slamming the knife into his back over and over. It's bloody and over the top, but that's Sisco for you. He thrives on blood and death. The man's back is a mess of torn flesh and gore and he's clearly dead, but still Sisco continues. Natalia clings to me, seeing the monster within Sisco for the first time.

I wonder, idly, if she regrets her decision to stay now.

Blood splatters his features and drips down his chest and arms as he continues on with the slaughter. He's eyeing the bodies, searching for someone else to kill, his arms raised, knife gripped tightly...

"Sisco!" Eva screams from somewhere in the house, and he stops and looks up at me, a crazed look in his eyes. "Sisco, where are you?" she sobs.

Blood drenches his hands and chest, and his face is dripping with it. We all know she'll be terrified if she sees him like this. She's used to blood and death, but she doesn't know that her oldest brother is a psychopath.

"I've got this," Natalia says softly, treading carefully across the room until she reaches the doorway. "Stay where you are, Eva," she calls up the stairs.

"I'm scared," Eva sobs from upstairs. "Dominic...

mom is coming."

"Do not let her come down here, Eva!" I warn. "Fuck," I say through clenched teeth.

"I want to come down," Eva whines.

"No, stay there!" Natalia says urgently. "You both need to stay up there."

I'm trying to think quickly, my brain running in all directions. If either of them see the bodies down here it will destroy them. Our mother will never recover from it. She barely recovered from seeing our fathers' mutilated body on the doorstep. And Eva? My sweet, innocent little sister...she's already seen too much blood and death for one lifetime.

"Remember when you told me about the special place where you hide sometimes?" Natalia continues.

"Yes."

"Go there now, take your mom. I'll come and get you both as soon as it's safe."

Eva is silent as she considers this, and I stare in amazement at Natalia. My sister has never let anyone get close to her, yet now I'm finding that they're sharing secrets. When I look at Joey he's grinning, his blood-splattered face looking like the cat that not only ate the canary, but its entire family too.

"Eva, did you hear me?" Natalia prompts, her tone sterner, demanding obedience. "Take your mom and go hide until I come and get you."

"Are you all okay?" She's crying softly and my heart aches that I've brought this into her home, again.

"Yes, of course. We're all fine. Now go hide, please."

"I'm going. Don't be long," Eva says, and then I hear her little feet running away. "Come on, mom," I hear her whisper.

Natalia turns and looks at us all, her gaze straying to the mass of bodies by her feet. She's standing there in my blood-soaked shirt, her hair a tumble of knots and waves around her shoulders, blood spattering her face, and her eyes wide as she takes in the destruction surrounding us, and all I can think about is taking her over my father's desk.

This woman has got me so twisted up I can barely think straight.

"Is this what it's like?" she asks us. "All the time?"

Joey heads toward her for damage control, but she holds a hand up in warning and he stops in his tracks. My heart is thumping in my chest so hard it hurts, and I realize I'm more terrified that she'll tell me that she won't stay than I was of armed men charging in our house to kill us.

"Not all the time," Sisco says with a shrug, like a fucking idiot.

Natalia is the mafia princess of Frank Costello, yet despite who her father was and the life she grew up in, she's been sheltered from almost all of it. Not to mention that no one would ever be stupid enough to take on Frank.

"Dom," Joey warns, and there's a desperate sort of pleading in his tone. He wants me to fix this, and I know that I have to because the only other way out of this situation will be Natalia chained up in our basement as my brother's sex slave for the rest of her life.

They meant it when they said they wouldn't give her up.

"Natalia," I soothe, my palms open beseechingly, but I don't know what else to say to her, or how to make this right. It's not just the pile of bodies at her feet. Or the monster she just saw in Sisco, from the madness that lives inside him. It's all of it and there's no way to save this situation.

Thankfully, I don't need to.

"It's...it's okay...I think," she says, letting out a slow, careful breath. "I can deal with this." She blinks rapidly and gives a nod. I can see that she's still shaking, but she seems so strong. So determined. I glance at Joey, seeing the look of pride on his face.

My brothers were right all along, she was made for us.

Sisco wipes a hand down his face, smearing the blood. He looks even more monstrous now but Natalia seems unfazed.

"I should change and then go and find Eva and your mom. They'll be scared," she says, her gaze darting between us all. "Will you..."

"This will be cleared within the hour," I promise her

immediately, and she nods satisfied by my answer. She turns to leave but Sisco's next words stop her in her tracks and she turns back.

"Brothers, have you seen this," he says, pushing one of the bodies out of the way to reveal a familiar face.

She gasps, her hand flying to her mouth as she looks from the deathly pale face and then up to all of us. "Oh my God. This is my fault," she sobs. "I'm so sorry."

"No, it's not," I say automatically as I come forwards.

Sisco rolls Alfonso over onto his back and his eyes stare up emptily.

"It is, it's my fault. You all could have been killed because of me. Eva could have been killed because of me . . . because of his jealousy." She's shaking, but I think it's as much anger as it is sadness, and there's something about that that makes me desire her even more.

"There are things you need to know, Natalia, but right now I need to get my men in here to clear this up. We will talk about this later and you'll understand that none of this was your fault," I say firmly.

"But—"

"Natalia," I warn, "go find my sister and keep her safe while we sort this mess out. That's an order."

Her eyes narrow at that last part and I can't help the devilish smile that comes to my face at the thought of her defiance.

"Do as I say now before I take you over my damn knee,

Natalia," I say with a firmer tone, "and it will not be for pleasure."

There's blood, bodies and bullets everywhere. It's not a new phenomenon for this office or this home. I was raised on hells grounds and we bathed our childhood in death and destruction. We had no choice then, but we do now, and I do not want Eva to become accustomed to this way of life.

My tone has the desired effect on Natalia, and she nods and leaves the room quickly. I pull my phone from my pocket and call in my cleanup team. This whole mess will be gone by morning.

Something dawns on me then, as I look around at the blank-eyed stares of the dead men at my feet, and I look across at my brothers.

"You know what this means?"

"Frank's gone," Sisco says, and glances at Joey.

"And now Alfonso is gone too," Joey adds.

I nod in agreement, the same conclusion drawing in their minds. "That makes us the new kings of the city, brothers."

They both smile widely, and I can't help smiling too, despite what we've just been through.

It was an ambition that our father had always had for us.

A pipedream, so to speak.

Only now it wasn't a dream, it was reality.

Myself and my brothers now ruled this city. With the three of us in charge, the world was our oyster and we would be unstoppable.

Things hadn't played out exactly how I'd expected them to, but the result was still the same. We were three brothers, the new three kings of the city, and with our queen by our side we were strong enough to take on anyone and anything.

Chapter 14

2 Months Later

Dominic

Natalia stares around at our new business venture with approving eyes and a smile on her face.

"You like it?" Sisco asks, keen for her approval.

"She likes it," Joey says arrogantly before looking hesitant. "You do, right?"

Pussy-whipped, both of them.

She stares around her, taking in the new casino we've purchased. She gives it an appraising look. Nodding and umming and aahing as she looks around. She's supposedly deep in thought, but I've already seen the twinkle in her eye to suggest otherwise.

Joey and Sisco watch with concern and I shake my head.

"Natalia, stop fucking with them," I growl, and she laughs, the sound making my dick twitch.

"I love it," she says with a smile. She reaches up on tiptoes and kisses each of them on the cheek. "And it's all legitimate?"

"Of course," Sisco agrees swiftly—too swiftly.

She puts a hand on her hip and raises an eyebrow at him.

My nostrils flare because I know I'm going to spank that look off her face later.

"It's mostly legit," I say, before Sisco says something stupid to fuck this up. "We are our father's sons after all."

She purses her lips and looks around at the casino we're standing in. "I love it," she says again, "and I love you." She kisses Sisco on the cheek, her hand briefly touching the back of his neck just the way he likes it. "And you." She kisses Joey, her hand smoothing down the front of his suit. "And you," she says before kissing my cheek.

I wrap an arm around her waist and tug her to me before pressing a rough kiss to her lips. I can't get enough of her. I pull out of the kiss and stare into her eyes, wondering if it was too early to fuck her over one of the tables and christen this joint. She sees the dirty look in my eye and swats at me and I smirk back.

"We have something else to show you, Natalia," I say,

allowing Joey to take her from me and guide her toward the back wall where an extravagant bar is. He looks over his shoulder at me with a smirk, already knowing that she's going to love it.

She gasps, noticing right away the framed photograph of her father hanging above the glittering bar.

I walk toward them all, my hands in my pockets as I stop and look at Frank staring down at us. Truth be known, I didn't want him there, but if it makes her happy . . . shit, maybe I'm pussy-whipped too.

Still, Frank doesn't deserve her love, and he doesn't deserve to hang on our casino wall. But then, in some ways, it's also a comfort to know that he will be there looking down at us, watching as our success grows and grows. Watching as his beloved daughter is shared between the three of us, his deepest enemies.

"Thank you so much," she says, her voice shaking like she might cry at any moment.

"Don't cry, little mouse," I say and she throws me a happy, tearful smile.

After everything she's been through, it was the least we could do for her. She didn't get the chance to take her vengeance out on Alfonso for killing her father, but I could help make sure his memory lived on. I could make sure that he got to see Natalia grow into the woman she should be.

Once we told her everything that had happened, the way

Alfonso had poisoned her father, Frank, trying to take him out of the game so he could take over the kingdom, and the way he'd failed the first time but unfortunately succeeded the second, I knew she'd never leave us.

She had nothing left but us. Regardless, I knew we were enough for her. And there wasn't anything that Natalia would ever want for again. I'd make sure of it.

And our father?

His killer?

Well, Frank got what was coming to him in the end anyway. It's a shame that Sisco never got to spend several months with him tied to his chair in the basement, but he still got a deserved ending. He knew that we had filthied up his beautiful daughter before he was murdered by Alfonso. The fact that it all worked out in our favor was just an added bonus.

But Natalia doesn't need to know that part.

Natalia turns and runs to me, throwing her arms around my neck. She stands on tiptoes and presses her lips to mine, kissing me passionately.

"Thank you, Dominic, you've no idea what this means to me," she says breathlessly, her hand going to the front of my pants and pressing against my hardening cock.

I glance over her shoulder as Sisco and Joey smile and come forwards, eager to join in.

"Show me then," I say and she nods, a smile on her face.

Natalia lowers herself to her knees, before unbuckling my dress pants. She looks up at me as she slides my hard length out before deftly wrapping her mouth around it. I groan in the back of my throat as her warmth envelopes me.

I reach a hand down and wrap it in her long mane of hair, fisting it, and she opens her throat up to my cock, allowing me deeper access. She sucks hard, pumping me steadily. Sisco and Joey stand on either side of her, their pants round their ankles and their cocks in hand, waiting patiently. She releases my cock, flicking the tip of it with her expert tongue before turning on her knees to Sisco and taking his cock in to her mouth.

He groans heartily, his hands in his hair as he fucks her mouth roughly, his gaze never leaving her. Eventually he reaches down and clasps the bottom of her chin, slowly sliding himself out of her hungry mouth and she turns to Joey.

Joey looks down at her with a soft smile and she takes him in her mouth. She sucks hard, her cheeks going hollow as she slides him in and out, and when he can't take anymore, he pulls himself out with a hearty rumble.

"Fuck, Natalia," he mumbles, holding a hand out to her.

She takes it and climbs back up to her feet. He guides her over to the nearest blackjack table, the one closest the bar and then hands her off to me with a wink. I bend her over the blackjack table, flipping her skirt up. I smooth a hand over her wet pussy, her panties already sodden.

"Please," she whimpers.

"Always so eager, little mouse," I say before gripping her panties and tearing them off in one quick movement, the silky material snapping easily. I line myself up at her entrance before sliding myself slowly into her.

She takes me, every thrust, every stroke, every hungry pound into her velvet pussy, and she finally comes with a cry as she squeezes my cock tightly and I come in hot spurts, drenching her insides. I step back, panting, my gaze on her perfect ass as I gather my wits. Sisco takes his place behind her and slowly slides himself into her. She whimpers and pants, her hands gripping the table as he fucks her quick and hard. He spanks her ass red. A spank with each thrust of his hips until he finds his own release minutes later. Sisco comes with a loud roar, the heavy table shifting forwards as he slams himself into her one last time, and she cries out. He grinds his hips, letting her pussy milk him dry.

Natalia looks back over her shoulder at him, her cheeks flushed from her second orgasm. He steps back with a satisfied grin, his hands still roaming her body as she stays bent over the table, eager and waiting for Joey.

"More," she whimpers.

Fuck me. I feel myself growing hard again and I knew I would never have enough of this beautiful, powerful woman. She has no idea the power she has over each and every one of us.

She was always so good.

Always so hungry for more.

Three men barely satisfied her, and that thrilled me in a way I couldn't explain.

Because the three of us would spend our lives trying to satisfy her.

Joey moves behind her, his cock hard and eager. He leans down and presses a kiss to her cheek. She swivels her head round to kiss him, her tongue darting out and sliding into his mouth.

"More, please," she begs him between kisses. "Please, Joey, I want more."

Joey pulls out of the kiss. He scoops up the cum from between her legs and smooths it over her asshole before lining his heavy cock up with her hole and pressing himself inside slowly. Millimeter by millimeter he pushes inside, stretching her slowly, filling her to the brim, until his full length was settled within her.

He waited several long moments for her body to adjust, Sisco and I growing harder as we watched Natalia's gratified expression. She bites down on her lower lip, her legs almost buckling. Joey lay his back over hers and slides the thin straps of her dress down so he can kiss her shoulders and neck, his hands reaching round to cup her breasts in his large hands.

"I'm going to fuck you now, Natalia," he whispers against her ear and she nods. Her gaze finds mine as Joey's hips begin to move, sliding his cock almost all of the way out of her. He pauses as his thick cock stretches her entrance, his hands on her hips to steady her and then with one heavy thrust he pushes back inside.

He moves with ease, his cock sliding in and out of her hungry, wanton body slowly at first. His hips rutting back and forth but picking up pace until he begins to chase his own release. Joey fucks her hard until she can't stand up and he has to physically hold her up so she doesn't collapse to the floor. Until orgasm after orgasm rolls through her repeatedly and her mouth is open in a silent cry as he seeks his pleasure. He fucks her, squeezing and pulling at her ass until finally he pulls out and comes in hot rivulets across her ass cheeks, giving a deep groan of satisfaction.

"Fuck, Natalia," he calls loudly.

Several long, breathless moments pass as we gather our thoughts and collect ourselves. Beads of sweat pepper my forehead and I dab at them as I release a slow breath.

"Jesus," Sisco says, zipping his pants back up.

"Well, I guess we just christened this joint," Joey finally says as he pulls a pocket square from his breast pocket and wipes his cum from Natalia's ass. He smirks, his heated gaze still on her perfect peach of an ass, no doubt already thinking of round two.

"Brothers, Natalia," I say, "I hate to be the one to break up the party, but we have a meeting to attend. Business is business and it waits for no man."

Joey grumbles and straightens himself. He pulls Natalia's dress back down over her ass and helps her to stand back up. Turning her in his arms, he leans down, pressing his lips against her forehead. She looks up at him when he pulls away, her doe eyes making my heart sing.

"Are you okay?" he asks and she nods subserviently as he lifts the straps of her dress back up to cover her perfect breasts.

Her cheeks are flushed, her chest still heaving. "I am now," she says breathlessly and we all chuckle. "Can I come to the meeting? Is it about the casino?"

Sisco steps forwards, gently tugging Natalia free from Joey's arms and into his own. "This is...a different type of business." He presses a kiss to her forehead and I can tell he wants to play with her again. The woman is never satisfied, and neither are we.

She frowns. "I thought you were legit now?"

Sisco tsks. "We said mostly." When she pouts unhappily he threads his hands into her hair and tips her head back so he can look directly into her face. "Do I need to spank that look off you, Natalia?" He eyes her hungrily, daring her, taunting her. Wanting her to test his patience. My cock begins to harden again.

A small smile rises on her face and now it's my turn to chuckle, drawing her attention away from Sisco to me. She raises an eyebrow questioningly.

"Always so eager," I say and Joey smirks. "All of you."

"And you're not, brother?" Joey asks moving to stand behind Natalia, his hands running up and down her arms. Her slight body is pressed between the two of them, completely at their mercy. She whimpers as Joey peppers her throat with kisses.

I would have loved nothing more than to sit back and enjoy the show, but we have more pressing matters to deal with.

"I can deal with this meeting on my own, if you'd like. I'll join the three of you later." I can feel my phone vibrating in my pocket and as eager as I am to strip Natalia naked and devour every inch of her perfect pink flesh, this meeting is especially important and can't be avoided.

Sisco glances across at me, obviously torn between duty and bloodshed and pleasure. Bloodshed always wins in the end and he reluctantly releases her from his grip. He sucks his lower lip into his mouth, releasing it with a frustrated pop.

"Later," he says, leaning down and pressing a hard kiss against her lips. He releases her mouth and looks over at me. "Let's get this done then, brother."

I nod, happy that he's made the right choice. I need his

specialist skills on this job. Alfonso may be dead, but his tiresome minions seem to be respawning. They want our heads for killing their king, instead, we're going to take theirs.

We're the kings of this city now, and we won't stand for their insolence.

"Natalia, Angelo will take you back home. A designer is meeting you at 2pm to discuss a new look for the casino. I trust you can oversee this for us." I smile, already knowing how much she'll be excited to do this and I'm not wrong.

Her eyes go wide, her concerns for bloodshed and war forgotten. "Oh my God, yes!"

She's happy.

We all are.

I've discovered that the two things seem to go hand in hand.

We stand there, the four of us, well fucked and happy, kings and queen of our city as the photo of Frank stares down at us. A sick sort of pleasure rolls through me that he got to see us defile his daughter just now. As he will for many years to come.

For Frank, this was the worst kind of torture.

And it would be never ending.

Epilogue

Natalia

Laying in bed on my own for the first time in months, I let out a satisfied sigh. I'd never known happiness could be like this. Never known what true happiness could be.

Until them.

Until Sisco, and Joey.

Until Dominic.

They are my everything. My world. And I am going to do everything in my power to make sure they know how much I love them. How grateful I am for everything they've done for me and given me.

I have a home. A family.

Eva, who I see as a little sister.

I have love and affection.

I have everything a girl could ask for.

Rolling on to my side, I throw back the covers and slip out of bed before heading to the bathroom to take a shower.

The brothers are at a business meeting this morning, but we're going for lunch this afternoon. Somewhere exquisite and expensive. They'll likely take me in the bathroom and leave a huge tip as an apology. The thought makes me smile and blush. Perhaps afterwards we'll do something fun too. The options are endless, though so were the responsibilities.

The casino would be opening in a few short months and they've tasked me with making sure it's ready for opening night. I've met with interior decorators and designed every inch of the place to perfection. Helped to interview staff. Arranged the grand opening. This was my baby, more so than it was theirs, and they make sure to tell me of this every single day.

These days I am far removed from the timid, kept princess of Frank Costello. These days, I am very much the busy, entrepreneurial soon-to-be-wife of the Novello brothers. I am busy and wanted and loved for who I am.

I step under the pounding water of the shower and lather up my long hair before rinsing it and smoothing conditioner through its long lengths. I wash myself thoroughly, noting the few bruises I have on my thighs and hips from the brothers' strong hands, and I smile, memories of the previous night flooding back.

Everything was as it should be, finally, and I breathe deeply in satisfaction at that knowledge.

I turn off the shower and step out, before wrapping a fluffy white towel around myself. Staring at my reflection, I smile, happy with the image that looks back. This woman, with her knowing eyes and smooth skin, she is everything I'd hoped she would become. Strong, powerful, determined.

She is everything a woman should be in this life, not weak and pathetic like my own mother.

I dress quickly and head back into my bedroom, giving a small squeak of surprise at the man standing by my bedroom window. He turns to face me, his expression hard and serious.

"Donny?" I whisper his name before rushing towards my bedroom door and slamming it closed. "What are you doing in here?"

My father's old security guard watches me with his intense gaze. I spin to him as he stalks forwards, his face stern.

"I did everything you asked," he says, his tone giving away his hurt.

"And I told you, you will be repaid for your loyalty." I tut and head to my dressing table to get myself ready. "You shouldn't be here. If they would have seen you."

He sighs heavily. "Natalia," he warns.

I glance behind me in the mirror, seeing his heartbroken expression and I feel a pang of guilt. Donny and a handful of my father's security have been employed by the brothers. I had assured Dominic that they were trustworthy, that their loyalty would be to me and now them. At first they hadn't been trusted, but slowly, they showed their worth, proved their loyalty. It was times like these though that I regret my decision to bring them with me.

"You need to go," I say and Donny's expression falls.

"I just...I needed to see you. I miss you." He places a heavy hand on my shoulder, my nipples automatically hardening at his familiar touch.

I look away from his pitiful stare.

I don't miss him.

I don't miss any of the men that had taken advantage of me.

All men, barring the brothers, had used me for one thing or another my entire life. I was a means to an end. Something to be bartered for or used. My father sold my innocence when I was just a baby, just so he could gain power. Did he really think that I would let that slide? That the daughter of the feared Frank Costello would not be strong enough to do something about his filthy betrayal?

And now here was Donny...another man that thought he loved me. Another man that wanted me for their own end. The good little wife. The breeder to bare their children.

They all made me sick.

"We'll be together soon," I lie. "I'm arranging everything."

It's scary how easily the lies slip from my tongue.

But scarier still how easily these men fall for the lies. How much power I hold over them.

Donny hadn't taken much persuasion to poison my father.

A token kiss.

A fumble in the dark.

It was almost sad how he thought I would ever give up my life to be with him. And then the brothers came along, and he still thinks I will give up my perfect life with them to be with him.

"Don't keep me waiting much longer, Natalia," he says, his tone darkening, "I've been patient enough."

"You have," I say, reaching up to touch his hand.

He lowers it, pushing beneath down my dress to cup my breast, kneading it in his huge hand. I sigh at his touch and he paws at me, hungry for me. I hold his gaze in the mirror as his other hand fumbles to undo his belt.

I'm already opening the drawer in front of me and pulling out my gun, and as he pushes down my dress I turn and fire my gun into his chest with familiar speed and accuracy. A skill that Sisco has taught me.

The bang from the gun is loud. The second one even louder.

Donny stumbles backwards and then falls, his hand going to his chest. To the red bloom that's growing there.

I stand up, kicking over my stool and gripping the front of my dress before yanking it hard enough to tear the material. Walking towards him, I stand looking down.

"I'm sorry," I say, and I am. That much is true. "But I won't let you ruin this for me, Donny."

"I love you," he gasps, his expression pained. He tries to sit up and I aim the gun at him again and shake my head.

"You don't," I insist.

"Natalia, I do, I love you," he wheezes, a mouthful of blood splattering across his paling face.

"I don't love you though." I fire into his chest again, this time, the ringing in my ears is loud, but I can still hear the telltale stomping of feet running towards my bedroom.

I drop the gun and crouch down low by my bed, forcing the tears out. The door is thrown open and Angelo and some of the other security come running in, their guns drawn. I cry out as they scan the room for dangers, quickly coming to the conclusion that Donny had been the only danger here and he is now dead.

Angelo comes to me, reaching out a hand to help me back up. "Are you okay?" he asks, his grey eyes assessing me quickly.

I nod. "I think so. He just...he said he loved me and then he tried to..." I cry. They aren't fake tears; they are real in every sense of the sadness I feel for one of my oldest friends.

I had loved Donny, but not like he had loved me, and nothing like the way I love the brothers.

They are my everything, and I know that I am theirs, and I will do anything to protect what we have and keep them happy and protected, no matter the consequences.

Dominic, Sisco and Joey may be the three Kings of this city, but I am their Queen.

The Queen, and I can rule just as well as them.

The end...at least for now.

Looking for more mafia romance?

Read on for chapter one of
~ BORN TO DARKNESS The Bratva Mafia Twins Duet ~
Deviant Prince #1

Deviant PRINCE

BORN TO DARKNESS
THE BRATVA MAFIA TWINS DUET

Claire C Riley

Deviant Prince

Born to Darkness

The Bratva Mafia Twins Duet

Heavy is the head that wears the Bratva crown.

Alexander Vasiliev carries the burden of his family's legacy

and his life must follow a singular path; Become his father,

King of the four criminal cells in their area.

A Pakhan.

The Boss.

The godfather of the Russian underworld.

Fierce ruler with a keen sense of business and unwavering

brutality.

His life is a cocktail of blood, death, and money.

But the weight of royalty goes hand-in-hand with certain

pleasures. And Alexander is an Alpha with an appetite.

He has everything he could desire. And more.

Until he meets her.

Marisha Zolotov.

She's off limits.

She's married to one of his father's powerful business

associates.

She's forbidden.

But that doesn't mean Alexander will take no for an answer.

He's used to getting what he wants, and he isn't about to let

her marriage get in his way.

Deviant Prince is the first installment of Born to Darkness, The Bratva Mafia Twins Duet. Followed by **Twisted Princess**.

Disclosure: Born to Darkness is a HOT, no-holds-barred, mafia romance with flavors of suspense and DOMs that leave you wanting more. Graphic sex. Language. Violence. Illicit dealings. Not for the faint of heart.

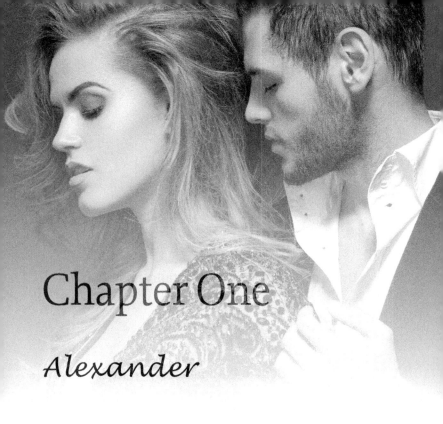

Chapter One

Alexander

He ruled with an iron fist and he wouldn't go easy on my uncle. We worked hard to build our empire and greed had no place in our circle. My uncle should have known better...

"Come, Eduard, let us drink and forget this," he waved a hand in the air, "we are brothers after all. A small mistake. A silly infraction." He waved his hand again, a slight tremor tracing through his fingers, and I sneered because I could sense my uncle's fear. It was palpable in the air.

We were all gathered in my father's office in our family home. Though 'home' was an understatement; the place was big enough to comfortably handle several large families within its infinite rooms and copious grounds.

My father sighed and stood up. He nodded as he moved around the large mahogany desk. His face was a mask, giving no sign of what he would do next. But I already knew.

Blood is thicker than water.

But disloyalty is a stain that won't come clean.

He stood behind my uncle's chair, putting his hands on his shoulders. "Brother, you disappoint me so," he said, before letting go with a heavy sigh. I knew in that moment that my father was letting go. Of the brotherhood that had defined his childhood. He would not embrace my uncle. He would not give him such a soft goodbye.

That wasn't the way of things.

There was no forgiveness, not for this kind of betrayal.

"It is not always so black and white, brother. It's not always that easy," my uncle replied. "You know this." There was no dark resignation in his tone. He still believed that the blood between them would save his life.

But he was damned.

In soul and body.

My father stood behind my uncle.

Posture straight, shoulders back, his mouth pulled in a tight line.

I picked up my glass, sipping on the vodka in it as my father pulled out his gun and fired a single bullet into the back of my uncle's head. Blood sprayed the desk and my uncle's head lolled forwards. My father sighed and shook his head and I raised an eyebrow.

"It is always that easy, brother," he said with a heavy heart. He looked across to me and I gave a nod of agreement. I saw the power in his eyes, and the pride on his face at my disciplined and unfazed expression.

"He was a traitor. He knew the consequences," I stated simply. I put down my glass as I stood up, straightening my suit jacket before buttoning it. I headed across the room, patting my father's shoulder as I went. "I'll have Damien come and clear the mess."

I gestured to my uncle's dead body with a wave of my hand.

"Thank you, son," he replied. "Are you coming tonight?"

I stopped in the doorway and turned to face him. "If you want me there, then of course I'm there," I smiled, "but if I'm not needed..."

He laughed. "Always the playboy, my son. Unfortunately, those days must end eventually. You'll need to find a wife soon enough, and there are many loyal families going to be there tonight, families with beautiful daughters. It would be good business for you to be seen. Perhaps someone will catch your eye there, or maybe you will catch someone else's eye."

"I'm not having your rich friends palm me off with one

of their daughters, father. A man should choose his own wife." It was the one thing we'd both agreed on; I would find my own wife with no interference from the family. Though, our deal didn't stop every rich Russian family from trying to lay their supposed virginial daughters at my feet.

I sighed, turning the platinum band on my right hand, the emblem of the family crown smooth under my fingers. Murder. Death. Violence. None of these things even made me blink, but the thought of marrying frayed my nerves.

My father laughed heartily. "Stop fearing the inevitable, son. A wife isn't so bad."

"Neither is a harem of women," I countered with a chuckle.

He barked out another laugh. "This is true, but a harem of women can't bring you an heir, and that is what we need to continue the family name."

He had me there. I raised an eyebrow and nodded. "I'll see you at the party, father."

"And I will see you, my son," he responded with a firm nod of his own. And the steel in his gaze spoke further than his words. My father and I might have a 'deal', but I couldn't put off marriage for much longer. There would come a time when he would choose a wife for me, if I refused to choose my own. The continued Vasiliev legacy was greater than either of us.

Leaving his office, I headed to my car--a sleek black

Maserati GranTurismo Sport. Before stepping out into the sunlight, I was already pulling my cell phone from my jacket to call my best friend, Nikolai. He picked up on the third ring, as the phone connected to my car after starting the engine; the rumble beneath me was satisfying and electric. It was the lifestyle I chased, the lifestyle I was clinging to...

The lifestyle that would drastically change once I was chained to a wife.

"Party tonight," I stated.

He laughed. "I'm not falling for that one again. This is some stuck-up family thing you're roping me into again, isn't it? I have a very good memory of the last time, Alexander."

I smirked at the memory. "One moment," I replied as I pulled out of my driveway, but almost immediately slowed to a stop again. Lowering my window, I gestured for Damien, the head of our family's security, to come over. Nikolai fell silent immediately.

"Alexander," Damien said as he approached, dipping his head in a show of deference.

"It's done. Get the body moved and the office cleaned," I ordered, and he nodded assent.

"I'm sorry," he offered, his face a picture of frustration, "I should have known. I could have stopped what was happening earlier."

I held a hand up to stop him. "No one could have known his treachery. What's done is done. Have the situation dealt with and my father's office spotless before we return home tonight, and all will be forgiven."

Damien nodded once again and stepped away from the Maserati. I rolled my window back up and continued to drive. For a normal person, someone not born into a world of darkness, what had just happened in my father's office would cause distress. They'd be emotionally distraught, unable to function.

For me, it was just another day. Just another death. I felt nothing.

"Now, where were we?" I asked, alerting Nikolai that he could speak.

"You were telling me about the crazy party we were going to tonight. Lots of women, lots of alcohol, and lots of drugs, yes?"

How did you guess? That's exactly how it will be." I laughed.

"Please tell me that there'll at least be some women our age? We don't have much longer before we'll be married with no time to have any fun," Nikolai whined.

Just like me, he was reluctant to marry. Yet we both knew it had to happen. And sooner rather than later. We both must follow in our fathers' footsteps, which meant an heir was needed to continue the bloodline. Of course, Nik had it easier. His father was dead, honorably so in service to the family. Though, my own father treated Nik like a son and both of our mothers were also eager to have us married. We'd been told all of our lives that our wives must come from good stock, whatever the fuck that meant. They had to be the products of wealthy, established families and one could only hope that they would be beautiful too.

Line the best stock up in an auction house and bid on them like cattle. The best breeder wins the hand of the Prince and his best soldier.

"There will be lots of women," I agreed, breaking from my thoughts.

"You swear?" Nik sounded like he trusted me about as far as he could throw me.

Which was not at all.

I laughed heartily. "Lots and lots of women, all ripe for our choosing."

It was one of the many benefits of being the son of the feared Eduard Vasilov and heir to his bloody, powerful throne; people were at my beck and call, and women were always primed for the taking.

Even at a boring-as-hell business function that I'd just tricked my de facto brother into attending with me in a bid to liven up the inevitable tedium.

One-click your copy now!

Add it on Goodreads here:
[Deviant Prince: Born to Darkness by Claire C. Riley | Goodreads](#)

Order book one DEVIANT PRINCE here:
US: https://bit.ly/37t2j00DeviantPrinceUS
UK: https://bit.ly/3q00ZysDeviantPrinceUK

Order book two TWISTED PRINCESS here:
US: http://bit.ly/2XUQbI8TwistedPrincessUS
UK: http://bit.ly/3bN16vETwistedPrincessUK

About the Author:

Claire C. Riley is a USA Today and International Bestselling author.

She lives in the United Kingdom with her husband, three daughters, and ridiculously naughty rescue beagle, Dogface. She loves dresses with pockets and is obsessed with 80's movies.

She is represented by Lane Heymont of The Tobias Literary Agency

Gryffindor. Targaryen. Zombie slayer.

Purchase links:
US Links: http://bit.ly/2O5rc0MClaireCRileyUS
UK Links: http://bit.ly/2XylLduClaireCRileyUK

Also by Claire C. Riley

Romantic suspense/thriller:
Beautiful Victim
Fragments of Delores

MC Romance:
Ride or Die a Devil's Highwaymen series
Nomad the Devil's Highwaymen Series:
Crank #1,
Sketch #2,
Battle #3,
Fighter #4,
Tame his Beast Duet (a Beauty & the Beast retelling set
in the Devils Highwaymen world)

Mafia Romance:
The Bratva Mafia duet co-authored with Ellie
Meadows:
Deviant Prince #1
Twisted Princess #2
Royal Blood: The Brotherhood (a RH mafia romance)

New Adult Romance:
Wrath #3 the Elite Seven Series

Contemporary Romance:
Shut Up & Kiss Me

Post-Apocalypse/dystopian romance:
Odium The Dead Saga series
Odium Origins Series
Out of the Dark
Red Eye: The Armageddon Series – co-authored with
Eli Constant
Thicker than Blood Series – co-authored with Madeline
Sheehan

Paranormal Romance:
Limerence. (The Obsession Series)
Limerence II (The Obsession Series)
Twisted Magic Raven's Cove

Horror:
Blood Claim

Available in paperback, eBook, and audiobook, and
Kindle Unlimited.

CONTACT LINKS:

Website: www.clairecriley.com

Claire C. Riley FB page: https://www.facebook.com/
ClaireCRileyAuthor/

Amazon: http://amzn.to/1GDpF3I

Reader Group: Riley's Rebels: https://www.facebook.
com/groups/ClaireCRileyFansGroup/

Newsletter Sign-up: http://bit.ly/2xTY2bx

IG: https://www.instagram.com/redheadapocalypse/

@ClaireCRiley